"Uncle. Uncle!"

He'd never heard the expression, but got the message. Out of breath himself, he closed the distance between them and took her hands to lift her upright. "I didn't hurt you, did I?"

"Only my pride that I had to surrender." She tilted her head back. The pure oval of her face glowed in the reflected starlight and snow. Her eyes danced with laughter.

He wanted to kiss her. Oh, how he wanted to enjoy a second embrace there in that quiet clearing. No one would interrupt them there.

Which was precisely why he let her go. He had no right to touch her, to disrespect her because they were alone and had enjoyed a quarter hour of play.

"Let me take you home." His voice was a mere rasp.

She nodded and tucked her hand into the crook of his elbow. They headed out in silence, save for the rhythmic crunching of their footfalls, yet the lack of conversation felt comfortable, companionable. Shared play, shared laughter were a powerful bond. So powerful a bond he feared he could too easily love her.

Perhaps he already did.

Books by Laurie Alice Eakes

Love Inspired Heartsong Presents

The Professor's Heart
The Honorable Heir

LAURIE ALICE EAKES

Since she lay in bed as a child telling herself stories, Laurie Alice Eakes has fulfilled her dream of becoming a published author, with twenty books in print. Besides writing, she enjoys giving inspirational talks, long walks and knitting, albeit badly. She lives in Texas with her husband and sundry animals.

LAURIE ALICE EAKES

The Honorable Heir

HEARTSONG
PRESENTS

Recycling programs
for this product may
not exist in your area.

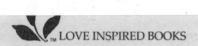 ™ LOVE INSPIRED BOOKS

ISBN-13: 978-0-373-48708-0

THE HONORABLE HEIR

www.Harlequin.com

Printed in U.S.A.

Have mercy upon me, O God, according to thy lovingkindness: according unto the multitude of thy tender mercies blot out my transgressions. Wash me throughly from mine iniquity, and cleanse me from my sin.

—*Psalms* 51:1–2

About Tuxedo Park

The latter decades of the nineteenth century were known as the Gilded Age, a time when scores of men catapulted into the ranks of the wealthy, often from humble roots. While these men made money, their wives and daughters strove to enter the upper echelons of New York society, which was fiercely guarded by the Astors, Vanderbilts and those who had ruled for decades. In short, this was the time when the American Dream really did come true.

Into this scene in 1885, Pierre Lorillard IV experienced his own American Dream. His family owned 4,000 acres in the Ramapo Mountains forty miles northwest of New York City, and he wanted to create an exclusive country retreat where his society friends could gather in the spring and autumn for the manly sports of hunting and fishing, and where ladies could join them at dusk for dinner and conversation.

Lorillard hired an architect named Bruce Price (father of Emily Price Post), imported hundreds of workers, and in less than a year, Tuxedo Park was born. Mansions, called "cottages," dotted the skirts of the lake, their manicured lawns perfect for croquet or badminton. Tuxedo Park offered a boathouse, stables, a private racetrack, stocked lakes, tennis courts, golf links, bowling lanes and hiking trails.

The most sought-after debutantes of every season came out at the Autumn Ball, a glittering event held each year around the first of November. The debutantes launched at Tuxedo Park were expected to make brilliant matches. Like the heroine of this story, many American heiresses sought after European titles, and at least four hundred acquired them and took hundreds of millions—billions in today's dollars—out of the country.

Emily Post's book, *Etiquette*, still used as a template for all that is gracious and socially correct, was first published in 1922. In this volume, she applied the manners and traditions she learned while growing up inside the fence that surrounded Tuxedo Park.

Chapter 1

The young widow should wear deep crepe for a year and then lighter mourning for six months and second mourning for six months longer. There is nothing more utterly captivating than a sweet young face under a widow's veil, and it is not to be wondered at that her own loneliness and need of sympathy, combined with all that is appealing to sympathy in a man, results in the healing of her heart. She should, however, never remain in mourning for her first husband after she has decided she can be consoled by a second.

Emily Price Post

Tuxedo Park, New York
November 1, 1900

She felt his gaze upon her from the instant she stepped into the clubhouse ballroom. That ballroom, all white pillars and blue velvet benches against the circular walls, fell silent the moment Catherine VanDorn, now Lady Bisterne, stepped through the doors from the great hall, and a hundred pairs of eyes swiveled in her direction. Yet the intensity of one man's bold stare drew her gaze past the gowns and jewels of the New York elite, to the audacious dark eyes of a gentleman at the far side of the room.

Her heart skipped a beat. Her gold-shod feet stumbled. The rainy November cold crept through to her bones, and for the first time that evening, she admitted that Mama, a yard behind her with Papa, was correct to tell her not to wear the mauve satin ball gown a mere thirteen months after her husband's death. It was too bright, too frivolous, proclaiming, however falsely, that the debutante who had departed from Tuxedo Park in triumph on the arm of an English lord, a scandal in her wake, intended to seek a new husband.

Behind her, her sister, Estelle, poked Catherine in the spine. "If I have to be here, at least let me in." She spoke in a whisper loud enough for the staring gentleman to hear.

The entrance unleashed a rising tide of exclamations, speculations, and a handful of greetings. "She doesn't look to be mourning anyone" came from a pretty matron in lavender tulle, and "I wonder whose fiancé she'll run off with this time" emerged from the pouting lips of a slip of a girl in white lace. But Mama's circle of intimate friends glided forward to embrace Catherine with wide sleeves and perfume and niceties like "I know your family is happy to have you here" and "You're too young to stay in blacks forever."

Pompadours and powdered cheeks blocked Catherine's view of the staring gentleman. Warmth began to steal back into her limbs, and she felt hopeful that perhaps she could make this homecoming work out well for everyone, especially her family.

She smiled back at the ladies, shook the hands of some older gentlemen, friends of her parents. Orchestra music rose from the stage, rising into an invitation for the annual ball to commence. Onlookers and interlocutors began to drift away in pairs to take their places in the center of the circular room. Catherine's parents strode off arm in arm, a young man claimed his dance with Estelle and their brother,

Paul Henry VanDorn III, claimed the hand of the doll-sized girl in white lace.

Catherine stepped back, her ruffled skirt brushing the blue velvet of a curving bench. She should seat herself and remain unobtrusive after her explosive entrée back into Tuxedo Park society. But sitting felt like surrender. Standing, on the other hand, looked too much as though she were inviting one of the still unattached gentlemen to ask her to dance. Indeed, two youthful men headed in her direction. She glanced away so she wouldn't meet their eyes as she had those of the man who had stared without subterfuge, but she found herself face-to-face with another issue.

"You aren't dancing, are you, Lady Bisterne." Delivering the question as a statement, an older lady who'd worn black for longer than Catherine's twenty-four years stomped forward with the aid of an amber cane and seized Catherine's hand in a crushing grip. "We may all recover from you returning in mauve, and perhaps even from the sight of those jewels in your hair, but if you dance tonight, you may as well take yourself back to England, as no one worth knowing will receive you."

Catherine granted the lady a curtsy. "I doubt you'll receive me regardless of whether or not I dance, Mrs. Selkirk."

"That depends."

"On what, ma'am?"

"Whether or not you're sorry for what you did to my granddaughter."

"Oh, I'm sorry if I hurt her. Perhaps she'll let me tell her just how sorry I am." Catherine looked for her old friend Georgette Selkirk, whom she had, in truth, done a favor by keeping her from marrying Edwin, the Earl of Bisterne.

She spotted Georgette gliding around the floor to the Strauss waltz—in the arms of the staring stranger. Georgette caught Catherine's eye for the merest heartbeat, then let her gaze flick away without acknowledging the look. A cut. A cut in front of most of the members of The Tuxedo Club. It may as well have been a slice to Catherine's heart.

In contrast, her companion caught Catherine's eye and inclined his head before the swirl of dancers carried him out of her sight again.

"Is that her new beau she's dancing with?" Catherine asked.

"A mere friend of my grandson's, but Georgette seems to have a growing fondness for him." Mrs. Selkirk rapped her cane on the floor dangerously close to Catherine's toes. "So keep your distance from Lord Tristram."

"Lord Tristram Wolfe?" Invisible hands seemed to have gotten hold of Catherine's stay laces and drawn them tight enough so that she could no longer breathe.

Mrs. Selkirk leaned forward to peer into Catherine's face, though she was a full head shorter. "Do you know him?"

"No, I never met him. But his cousin was with my husband when he died."

And if she didn't get away from Mrs. Selkirk's overwhelming scent of peppermint and the crowded ballroom, Catherine was going to expire right there.

"If you will please excuse me, ma'am…" Catherine slid a few inches over in preparation for gliding out of Mrs. Selkirk's reach. "I should ensure my sister's instruments have gotten stowed away behind the stage safely." She added a smile. "Would you like to sit for the upcoming performance?"

The cane thumped on the floor loudly. "I'd like you to assure me you won't hurt my granddaughter again."

"On the contrary, I wish to make amends for the past. May I call on your family in the near future?"

"I don't want you near our house."

The clipped words resounded like a blow to Catherine's heart.

She winced, blinking against blurriness in her eyes, and half turned away. "Then I'll be on my way." Without waiting for a fare-thee-well or permission to depart the woman's company, Catherine swept around fast enough to send the green velvet ruffles on the bottom half of her skirt flaring out like a dozen fans.

With Estelle swooping around the ballroom, Catherine did need to ensure her younger sister's instruments had reached the clubhouse. Being allowed to provide part of the night's entertainment, along with some of the other young people from Tuxedo Park, was the only reason Estelle agreed to attend the ball launching her into society. But if so much as a fingerprint marred the cello, violin, or the banjo especially, Estelle would leave, even if she had to walk uphill to Lake House through the rain. Having endured enough trouble getting Estelle to the festivities, Catherine was not about to let her younger sister behave with even a hint of scandalous behavior.

She slipped around a group of gawking young men she didn't recognize and headed for the doorway.

"Heed my warning." Mrs. Selkirk's voice rang out in the sudden lull as the waltz concluded.

She would have to find another way other than a social call in order to talk to her old friend Georgette. Right now, she needed to escape from Mrs. Selkirk and the folly of her imprudent decision to wear mauve and green to announce she had left first mourning several months early.

"Lady Bisterne." A drawling English voice cut through the hubbub of the throng—an all too familiar voice.

Her heart lurched in her chest like a badly sprung carriage. She halted and turned toward Ambrose Wolfe, for not doing so would be insufferably rude. He strode toward her with two other gentlemen in tow, one being Florian

Baston-Ward, the younger brother of the cousin who inherited her husband's estate, and the other the man who had been dancing with Georgette. Even if his looks likely opened any door he wanted, his choice of friends didn't recommend him as someone she wanted to meet.

Before them, the company parted as though the men were royalty.

"What are you doing here, Ambrose?" In as chilly a voice as she could muster, she addressed the man who had called to her, the man who had been with her husband when he died.

He stopped before her and bowed. "I had an invitation to visit this fair land of yours, so I took advantage of it."

"How nice for you." Her tone was sweet, though her stomach churned. "And you didn't come alone."

Ambrose's teeth flashed in a grin. "You know I never liked being alone."

Neither did she, but she had been for too many years thanks to men like Ambrose Wolfe.

"I have my cousin with me." He gestured to the stranger. "Lord Tristram Wolfe."

She'd never met the younger son of the Marquess of Cothbridge, but she'd heard of him in less than favorable terms. He was rather better looking than the gossip rags led her to believe. Actually, he was rather better than good-looking, with high cheekbones, a square jaw and eyes the color of fine dark Chinese jade, in perfect contrast to hair the color of caramel sauce with a rather delightful cowlick.

"Pleased to finally meet you, my lady." Lord Tristram bowed.

"How do you do?" She dropped a perfunctory curtsy, then glanced at her husband's cousin, Florian Baston-Ward.

He sidled closer to take her gloved hand and raise it to his lips. "Cousin Cate, I see you've come out of mourning already, complete with wearing stolen Bisterne jewels."

* * *

Later, Tristram decided, he would take Florian to task for tipping his hand regarding the jewels. For now, he would save his concentration for the lady and how she responded to the careless remark.

"Stolen?" Other than that single word and a widening of her long-lashed eyes, Lady Bisterne gave no telling reaction. Her complexion maintained its porcelain purity. No color drained from her cherry-ice-colored lips, and her gaze remained fixed on Florian's face.

In short, she didn't look guilty, despite the fact that two of the jeweled pieces Tristram had crossed half of Europe and the Atlantic to find shimmered and sparkled against her glorious dark auburn hair.

"Not a discussion for the ballroom." Tristram tore his regard from the lady to scowl at the younger son of his mother's cousin and his father's oldest friend. "Badly done of you, Baston-Ward. You should ask her to dance, not make careless accusations."

"I'm not dancing," she said at the same time as Florian exclaimed, "You expect me to ask her to dance? It's bad enough she's wearing colors—"

"Florian, be nice." Ambrose punched the younger man in the shoulder.

"Go foist yourself off on some pretty American girl," Tristram added, hoping to be rid of the youth so he could have a moment alone with Lady Bisterne.

Florian's blue eyes flashed with lightning. "When she left me penniless?" He waved a hand toward her ladyship. "No American girl would be interested in me."

"Try a wallflower." Tristram glanced around to locate the inevitable row of young ladies with whom no one wished to dance, either because of their poor looks or lack of money.

A lack of money wasn't prevalent in the land of the

wealthy elite, though some plain-faced young women did perch on the edges of the cushions as though about to jump up and run. Others lounged back as though they wanted to sit out the dance. One of the latter wasn't plain-faced at all. Indeed, she looked very much like Lady Bisterne.

"I see any number of young ladies not dancing." Tristram jostled Florian's elbow to get him thinking with reason about going away.

Florian opened his mouth as though to protest, then shut it again and stalked off toward the wallflower row. Ambrose followed with a mumbled, "Wouldn't mind another dance or two myself."

Tristram turned back, but Lady Bisterne had gone. She'd been heading for the door when Ambrose waylaid her. Tristram knew he should follow her in the event she disposed of those bejeweled combs in her hair. Not that doing so would change the fact that a hundred people had seen her wearing them as if she possessed a right to do so.

Tristram's mouth hardened and he headed for the exit. The sooner he learned the truth from her ladyship, the sooner he could return home and settle matters with his father. Only a little matter of first recovering the Bisterne jewels, and then explaining to her ladyship that if she didn't also pay back the money spent to recover those jewels, everyone in English and New York society would learn of her crime against her late husband's family. Simple tasks in the planning. At best difficult in execution.

"You're not going to go hide away with the old men, are you, Tris?" His host, Pierce Selkirk, clapped Tristram on the shoulder. "Never used to be the type to drink spirits and smoke cigars."

Tristram shuddered. "Not in the least." His lack of enthusiasm for such things remained, though it hadn't gone over well with his fellow army officers. "I simply wished to…"

He trailed off, unwilling to admit he was going after a

lady. Ambrose and Florian knew why he was in Tuxedo Park but as far as Pierce, his friend from university, was concerned, he was doing what titled men from all over Europe had been doing in the past decade or two—looking for an American heiress as a wife.

Not that he would object to marrying an heiress if he loved her. But his priority was to find proof that Lady Bisterne had stolen the jewels from her late husband's family in order to appease his father and prove he could succeed at something, having failed to bring military glory to the family.

Pierce was watching him with one sandy brow raised in enquiry, and Tristram struggled for a truthful response. "I wish to avoid another dance so soon." He touched the back of his head, where his hair now sprang up in an unruly cowlick from a ridge of scarring beneath.

"Ah, the old 'head not up to more twirling about'?" Pierce laughed. "Mine doesn't like it much, either, and I don't even have your excuse. But no need to worry. After this dance, there'll be an entertainment. Some of the younger set will perform."

"Sounds like a good reason to escape."

"Miss VanDorn, however, is a true talent." Pierce's gaze flicked to the dance floor where the auburn-haired young lady who resembled Catherine was whirling about with Florian.

"She's an extraordinary talent, actually," Pierce added.

"And pretty. Do I detect some interest there?" Tristram smiled.

"About as much as you have in my sister Georgette."

Tristram's smile died as the music ended. Dancers and chaperones cleared from the dance floor and politely jockeyed for seats on the blue velvet benches along the walls. Georgette, Ambrose and Florian joined Tristram and Pierce near the doorway.

"Miss VanDorn is one of the performers." Florian's eyes gleamed. "She plays the banjo. I've never heard one."

"They're all the rage with the ladies here." Pierce grimaced. "Most should burn theirs."

Both Florian and Ambrose protested such a notion, being musicians themselves.

"Pierce is referring to my attempts." Georgette's sweet voice held a laugh. "But Estelle is quite different. You'll enjoy her part. Now, do excuse me. I see Grandmother beckoning to me."

The old lady was waving her cane in their direction, much to the peril of those around her.

"She's going to brain someone with that one day." Pierce laughed.

Lights in the ballroom darkened as a hush fell over the ball, and several young ladies in fluttery white dresses filed onto the stage escorted by young men with dark coats and stiff collars. From behind them, an unseen musician gave them a pitch, and the chorus began to sing in voices angelic enough to grace any church.

A theatrical sketch followed the ballads. When she forgot her lines, the leading lady dissolved into nervous titters. As though this were part of the drama, the audience laughed with—or perhaps at—her. Someone prompted her from the rear of the stage, and she proceeded without another hitch.

"How long does this go on?" Ambrose whispered a little too loudly.

Tristram elbowed him in the ribs. "You'll never catch an American wife if you are rude."

"I'll never catch an American wife without a title," Ambrose countered. "Even your poor excuse of a courtesy title is worth something here."

Several people nearby hushed him.

The attention of the guests shifted from polite to inter-

ested as Estelle VanDorn glided onto the stage and settled
a peculiar-looking stringed instrument onto her lap.

She played like a professional musician. The notes
hummed and trilled and tumbled over one another like
gemstones caught in a waterfall. At the conclusion of each
piece, the audience applauded with the enthusiasm the performance deserved. After three selections, Estelle rose,
bowed, then swept off stage.

Lights from the chandeliers overhead blazed through
the room as voices rose to fill the circular chamber. On the
stage, the orchestra returned, while on the dance floor, the
guests began to mill about and again pair off into couples.

Ambrose punched Tristram's arm. "Time to start solving your mystery, Sherlock Holmes."

Tristram shook his head. "There is no mystery here. I
need to gather my proof or we can take no action against
even an American dowager countess."

He scanned the room for the countess. Surely she had
returned to hear her sister's performance. With his height
advantage, he should have been able to see her. But no jeweled combs flashed in dark reddish-brown hair. Tristram
began to leave the ballroom in search of Lady Bisterne.

"Oh, no, you don't, Lord Tristram." Georgette swooped
up beside him, her sky-blue eyes sparkling. "We need all
the men to continue partnering the debutantes. Let me introduce you."

Whether cool matron or giggling girl, one factor the
women shared in common was their reaction to learning
Tristram could, by way of his father's status, place *Lord*
in front of his first name. Their smiles widened, their fans
fluttered faster and they leaned a little closer.

Weary of Georgette Selkirk shepherding him forward
like a lost lamb, Tristram chose a plain but lively young
lady to be his partner in the first set. Miss Hudock ex-

ecuted the figures of the dance with light steps and not a
great deal of chatter.

"You've likely already seen what Tuxedo Park has to
offer, my lord, so do tell me about where you live. Is it a
castle?"

Tristram laughed. "It's rather a larger and older version
of many of the houses I see here in the Park."

"How old?"

"Three hundred and twenty years." He talked as they
rounded the circular ballroom.

"It belongs to my father, though, not to me." As he spoke,
he scanned the room for Lady Bisterne or her sister, curi-
ously still not seeing them. "The windows are rather gray
because the glass is so old."

"Will it be yours one day?"

"Not if God and I see eye to eye on the issue."

The young lady's gray eyes widened. "You don't want
to own a manor house?"

Only for the good he could do with the income, he
thought.

"Sometimes," he admitted. "A great deal of responsibility and privilege comes with it."

"My papa says privilege is a form of responsibility."

"You have a wise papa." Tristram bowed as the music
ended, and when he straightened, he caught a glimpse of
mauve satin through a door near the stage.

With more haste than the charming lady deserved, he
returned her to her mother, then skirted the room as quickly
as he could manage without knocking anyone over.

When he reached the doorway, he didn't see a sign of
her ladyship's luxurious gown. He did, however, catch a
glimpse of something sparkling against the floorboards.

In two strides, he reached the gemstones and scooped
them up. Diamonds sparkled, and gold and pearls gleamed
against his white glove. Above the teeth of the comb, the

setting arched on a twist at the edges, an unusual design brought into the Bisterne family over a hundred years earlier. The combs belonged to the estate, to the new Earl of Bisterne, his father's oldest friend. Yet the twenty-four-year-old Dowager Countess of Bisterne calmly walked off with them, as well as a host of other jewels that did not belong to her.

Tristram curled his fingers around the comb until the filigree setting and stones marred his gloves. Eyes narrowed, he scanned the corridor for her larcenous ladyship.

"I'll find you before you can rid yourself of the other comb." He headed down the great hall, which was nearly empty. Despite Georgette's claims, most of the men hadn't yet abandoned the ladies in pursuit of more manly diversions.

But her ladyship appeared to be quitting the festivities. Tristram spotted her on the other side of the massive fireplace, on her way toward the clubhouse's front door.

He started after her. A few couples strolled about, impeding his progress and line of sight. He paused, his way blocked by a cluster of young people. "I beg your pardon, but may I please get through?"

"We're terribly sorry." They started back.

Tristram lengthened his stride as he passed by. "Lady Bisterne," he called, keeping his voice low.

She either didn't hear him…or chose to ignore him.

"My lady?"

She grasped the faceted crystal doorknob.

Tristram closed his free hand over hers, feeling the chill of her fingers through their thin gloves. "I wouldn't do that if I were you."

She gasped and reared back. Her other comb lost its anchor on her hair and dropped to the floor with a clatter.

"What are you doing?" She yanked her hand free and

clapped her hands to her hair, still anchored by pearl-headed pins.

"I need to talk to you about this." He held out the first comb, then stooped to collect the other.

She set her foot upon it. "These were a wedding present from my late husband. That is all you need to know."

"That's not what the new earl claims."

"The new earl may—" An odd crunch sounded loudly enough to be heard over the orchestra and dancers. Her ladyship drew her brows together above a nose falling just short of perfect, took a step back and stared at the floor.

Where an elaborate hair ornament of diamonds and pearls had lain but moments earlier was now a twisted gold setting and pile of shards so small they came close to qualifying as dust.

Chapter 2

The groom buys the handsomest ornament he can
afford—a string of pearls if he has great wealth, or
a diamond pendant, brooch or bracelet, or perhaps
only the simplest bangle or charm—but whether it is
of great or little worth, it must be something for her
personal adornment.

Emily Price Post

Catherine felt as if she were floating somewhere over
her body, as she stared at the crushed, obviously artificial
gems on the floor, part of her listening to music, voices
and laughter, part of her aware of the sandalwood warmth
of the man before her. Beneath her, the heels of her shoes
seemed to have come loose, and she swayed.

Warm, strong hands closed over her shoulders. "Are you
going to faint, my lady?"

"I've never fainted in my life." She raised her hands to
press her palms on either side of her head. "I am not going
to faint over a little bit of deception on my husband's behalf. It won't be the first time I caught him in a lie." A bub-
ble of laughter rose in her throat. She gulped it down, and
tears filled her eyes. "Excuse me. I need some air." She
pulled free of his hands on her shoulders, flung open the
door too quickly for him to stop her and propelled herself
onto the porch.

The mist had turned to rain. It fell in cold and steady ribbons beyond the sheltering roof. She shivered, took a deep breath of the bracing air—

And remembered her sister.

"Estelle. Oh, no, I need to find Estelle. She didn't return to the ballroom after her performance."

Lord Tristram joined her on the porch. "It's too cold and wet out here for anyone to linger." He touched Catherine's elbow. "Come back inside. I'll help you find your sister. Could she have rejoined the dancers while you were in the hall?"

"I don't know. She promised me she'd stay. If she's run off into this rain—" She made herself take a deep breath. "One of Estelle's friends said she saw her heading for the door."

Catherine wouldn't doubt for a minute that her younger sister was perfectly capable of convincing the coachman to take her home. She might even take advantage of the family being occupied at the ball to carry out a threat she'd made upon Catherine's arrival home.

I want to run away and be on my own like you did.

She didn't seem to understand that, for Catherine, "running away" meant being a wealthy and titled female traveling across Europe with her lady's maid, an acceptable activity for a new widow. But a young lady did not run off on her own to join a group of musicians.

"I expect once she saw the weather," Lord Tristram said, "she would have gone back inside."

"That's what a sensible person would do, but Estelle is not sensible." Catherine turned back toward the door, sensible enough herself to get in out of the rain.

Lord Tristram opened it for her. She swept over the threshold and caught the glitter of paste gemstone fragments scattered across the floor by long skirts and shoes. Those fragments were all that remained of the gift that held so much promise for an eighteen-year-old girl with little sense and lots of vanity. They were another lie, another disappointment, another shattering of a dream.

And Florian Baston-Ward, her late husband's cousin, had accused her of taking the jewels. She must put a stop to such a rumor or her family would suffer. But if Estelle ran away, her family would also suffer.

If some ancient warrior suddenly appeared in the corridor with a battle-ax and sliced her in two, Catherine doubted she could feel more divided. Stop Florian from spreading his accusations, or find Estelle?

"Find Estelle," she said aloud.

"I'll help you, my lady."

"Why?"

He shrugged. "Why not?"

"The reasons are numerous. Because you are a stranger. Because you're an English aristocrat. Because you and your friends rather accused me of stealing Bisterne jewels."

"All that aside, a missing young lady is still a missing young lady."

Catherine gazed into eyes rimmed in gold-tipped lashes that lent them a sunny, warmth. Soft, gentle eyes that did not flinch away from her direct stare even after what she had just said.

"All English noblemen and their sons are not created equally, Lady Bisterne." His voice, with its clear, precise speech borne of generations of careful breeding and training, still managed to sound as gentle as his eyes appeared.

She felt a little warm. Her mind settled its frantic rushing from one crisis to another, and her spine felt straightened by more than her corset.

"Thank you." She glanced through the ballroom doorway. The dancers spun by in a graceful kaleidoscope of color, with the orchestra soaring in the background. "She likes to talk to members of the orchestras and bands at these galas."

"She's a talented young lady."

"She is. But she wasn't with them. And I don't see her in the ballroom. She's tall enough she usually stands out."

"And I'm tall enough I can usually see what I'm looking for."

He stood a full head taller than she even in her heeled evening slippers.

"Where else might she have gone?" Lord Tristram glanced at the staircase. "Upstairs?"

"It's a good place to start." As she headed for the steps her toe kicked something on the floor. Gold flashed as the filigree setting of the comb sailed across the hall. She grasped the newel post with one hand and swallowed against a burning in her throat. She could not accept that the gift she cherished through all those lonely years of her marriage turned out to be a fake.

Lord Tristram stooped and retrieved the bit of mangled gold. "We'll talk about this later."

"I have no idea why I should talk to you about my husband's perfidy." To form her response, she employed all the hauteur she had learned in her four years as the wife of a peer.

"I think you will," he responded calmly.

For a moment, their eyes met, and held. His remained calm and warm. She hoped hers conveyed that he should kindly remove himself from her presence. Since he remained right where he was, she concluded she must have failed.

She couldn't waste more time on him. As if he weren't following her, she turned and headed up the wide, polished treads once used for indoor tobogganing, until some young lady had shown too much petticoat lace and a young man commented on it. Ah, the silliness of youth.

The silliness of youth—Estelle's—kept Catherine climbing to the second floor, where there were private rooms for gentlemen withdrawing to smoke their cigars, and young ladies needing a place for their maids to repair a torn flounce or pin up a tumbled lock of hair. Catherine opened a door wide enough to peek around the edge. Two maids stood in anticipation of someone entering for assistance.

"Has Miss VanDorn been in here?" Catherine asked.

"No, ma'am." The maid bobbed a curtsy. "I haven't seen her tonight."

Catherine thanked her and closed the door. Lord Tristram had vanished from sight. Good. Estelle was none of his concern. Catherine's artificial jewels were none of his concern, either. She could not imagine why he'd acted as though they were.

She glanced up and down the passage. It remained empty—empty, but not quiet. Music from the ballroom soared from below along with the constant rise and fall of conversation and laughter. The rumble of male voices and the stench of smoke seeped from beneath a door farther down the hall. Estelle would never set foot inside there, even if the men allowed her to.

Catherine proceeded to the rooms she truly feared Estelle might occupy—ones not officially employed for the evening. If she had sneaked into one to hide and practice her music, not much harm would have been done. But Estelle wasn't above collecting musicians to accompany her, regardless of who the person was and with little regard to propriety. Few Tuxedo Park residents played music seriously enough for Estelle, so she took advantage of whom she could.

In a lull in the music and conversation below, from a chamber down the hall, bows drew across a cello and violin. Just then, Lord Tristram stepped into the corridor and beckoned to Catherine.

She closed the distance between them. "Is she in there?"

He raised a hand and flattened his cowlick. It sprang back the instant he removed his hand. "She…is." His unflappable demeanor seemed to have deserted him.

As butterflies fluttered in her middle, Catherine said, "And she's not alone."

"No." His tone held an odd note of annoyance.

Catherine reached for the door.

Lord Tristram opened it for her. "Lady Bisterne." He announced her as though he were a butler and she arriving at afternoon tea with a duchess.

The cello ceased. Its owner stood, and Catherine flung out one hand to grip the doorframe. "Florian?"

He bowed. "The same, my lady."

And just beyond Florian, Ambrose stood bowed as well, a violin tucked under one arm. Between them, Estelle remained seated, her banjo perched on her lap, her lips curved in a smile of satisfaction. For several moments, they stood like posed mannequins, then Catherine broke the tableau.

"What are you doing in here alone with two gentlemen you scarcely know?"

Estelle sighed. "If someone wishes to play music, what does formality matter?"

"Propriety." Catherine resisted the urge to snatch the banjo from her sister and take it someplace where she couldn't retrieve it. "And your word. You promised me you would stay for one set of dances after the performance."

"I did." A dimple appeared in Estelle's right cheek. "I didn't promise I'd dance."

Someone snickered.

"We will discuss this when we are not in front of strangers." Catherine shifted her gaze from her sister to one gentleman and then the other.

Ambrose and Florian refused to meet her eyes. Beside her, Lord Tristram stood with his mouth set in a grim line.

"I do believe," he said, "my fellow guests have forgotten their manners."

"Considering how Florian greeted me," Catherine said, "I believe he didn't come with his this evening." She took a step toward her cousin by marriage. "Tell me, why did you accuse me of stealing those jeweled combs?"

"I recalled them from the family jewels that belong to the estate." His gaze went to her hair. "They, like the rest of the jewels, went missing with Edwin's death…and they seem to be missing now. What did you do with them?"

"Lord Tristram has one." Catherine steeled herself against the pain of betrayal reawakened. "And I broke the other."

"So long as it can be repaired—" Florian began.

Catherine shook her head. "It can't be repaired. I stepped on it, and the jewels smashed."

Florian paled. "They were artificial?"

"As useless as library paste," Lord Tristram interjected.

And with that, Ambrose Wolfe's bow went sailing across the room to crack against the wall.

If it weren't for the din of the party, the withdrawing room at the top of the Tuxedo Park clubhouse would have been quiet enough to hear a mouse scuttling through the cellars. Silent and still.

Tristram observed his companions regarding one another, while avoiding meeting anyone's eyes. If not for those shifting gazes, they would have resembled a staged tableau or a set of scolded schoolboys.

As the eldest at twenty-eight, Tristram should break the stalemate. On the other hand, Lady Bisterne, as the social superior in the room, held the right to do so. She might not realize that fact, even after four years in England and another on the continent of Europe.

If she did know and chose not to end the impasse of

wills and Tristram took matters into his hands, he would be insufferably rude.

How long the five of them would have sat or stood like salt sculptures Tristram didn't know, for in the corridor, someone laughed. Lady Bisterne startled, and her hand hit the door, slamming it all the way shut. Everyone jumped.

Ambrose laughed and retrieved the broken bow. "So how do I go about replacing this?"

"In the city." Estelle began to pluck soft notes from the strings of her banjo. "Tuxedo Park is sadly lacking in music."

"Not with you here, Miss—"

"Florian." Tristram snapped out the younger man's name to stop the flattery. "Lady Bisterne and Miss VanDorn do not need you interfering here. You, either, Ambrose. We should repair to the ballroom."

"And dance with young ladies who won't look twice at me because I don't have a title?" Ambrose's lips turned down at the corners.

"They would if they heard you play the violin." Miss VanDorn gave him a positively worshipful look.

Lady Bisterne touched her gloved fingertips to a loose strand of hair fluttering charmingly over one ear, shook out the skirt of her gown as though it were coated in dust, then stepped forward, her head high, her chin thrust out and her shoulders drawn back. "Put your instruments away and bid good-night to these gentlemen." Her clear, deep blue gaze flicked from Florian to Ambrose. "I use the term as a courtesy, as you're considered gentlemen in England. Here, however, you have not behaved like gentlemen in coming to this room alone with a young lady. Do not do anything of the like again."

"Catherine." Miss VanDorn's face flamed. "You have no business in scolding them."

"Actually," Tristram said, "she does, as the social superior in this room."

"This is America. We don't hold with such ceremony." Miss VanDorn began a complicated finger-picking pattern on her five-stringed instrument. "We believe in equality."

"Which is why half the debutantes in the country want to marry European titles," Ambrose teased.

Tristram glared at Ambrose. "Enough, cousin." He bowed to her ladyship. "I'll take care of this riffraff if you wish to see your sister."

"Thank you." Lady Bisterne smoothed out a wrinkle in her glove, then tapped her fingers against the fragile wrist beneath. "Estelle, put up your banjo and return to the ballroom."

Miss VanDorn continued to play. "You know I detest dancing. Of all the men who've asked me to dance tonight, these are the only two with any sense of timing."

"We'll sign your card for the rest of the night." Ambrose and Florian spoke in unison.

They sounded so absurd, so young and eager, that Tristram laughed. "I think that would prove unacceptable."

"Indeed." Lady Bisterne's chin edged higher. "But they may escort us downstairs and carry the instruments."

Ambrose and Florian jumped to comply.

Tristram's gaze flicked to Lady Bisterne's expressive chin, where a dimple lay. It appeared as though a fingertip had pressed into the mold of her features to keep them from appearing too perfect, to give them character. Tristram's forefinger twitched as though he would trace that flaw and test the porcelain smoothness of her complexion.

He tucked his hands behind his back. "You lads should dance with Miss Selkirk, you know."

"To get her away from you?" Florian grinned.

Lady Bisterne paled. "I forgot you are staying with the

Selkirks. You had best go do your duty by Georgette. I will assist Estelle."

"You can't carry a cello downstairs any more than I can." Estelle's glance was scornful. "Mr. Baston-Ward and Mr. Wolfe shall assist me since it's not either of them Georgette is interested in."

Lady Bisterne's complexion appeared paler than the pearls around her neck, and she stooped to gather up the broken bow, her skirts billowing around her like petals.

"Do help the ladies, you two." Tristram looked at the pieces of the bow and opened his mouth to ask Ambrose why he had broken it, then silenced himself. He could talk to his cousin at any time regarding his poor behavior. Not so Lady Bisterne. Instead of nonsensical notions of touching that dimple in her ladyship's chin, he must remind himself that she was the reason for his presence in Tuxedo Park, New York. She was his prime suspect and he needed to talk to her in an environment where they would not be distracted or interrupted, which was not easy with everyone indoors in this inhospitable climate in November. Country walks proved far more convenient for private dialogue, but not in freezing rain.

He might get the opportunity momentarily, however, for with alacrity, Ambrose and Florian began replacing the violin and cello in their cases, and Miss VanDorn did the same with her banjo. Lady Bisterne stood staring at the broken bow as though not certain what it was or what to do with it.

Tristram took a step toward her, his intention to ask her if they could talk.

She thrust the bow at Ambrose. "Estelle and I will go before you two, lest our reputations suffer." She strode to the door, beckoning to her sister.

Slowly, Miss VanDorn followed.

Her ladyship was right. He couldn't talk to her there. Eagerness to solve this problem with the jewels and get away from Tuxedo Park before Georgette got her hopes raised in his direction were clouding his good sense.

He reached the door before Lady Catherine did and touched her arm. "May I call upon you tomorrow, my lady?"

"Call?" She patted at her hair where one of the combs had helped pearl-headed pins hold up her masses of glossy waves. "If you intend to explain your ridiculous charges, then yes, you may. Eleven-thirty. We shall be able to speak privately."

"Thank you." Tristram bowed and opened the door. "Good evening, ladies. If we do not see you in the ball-room, we shall see you tomorrow." He closed the door after them, then leaned against it, his arms crossed over his chest. He glared at Ambrose and Florian. "What were the two of you thinking? You know better than to be alone with a young lady."

"We found a way to get into the good graces of a pretty heiress," Florian said.

"We aren't heirs to a fortune and title, like you are," Ambrose added.

Tristram reminded him, "I am not an heir to a title if my brother's widow bears a male."

And if he did not restore the Bisterne jewels to the family, as well as recover the money the marquess was spending to recover those jewels, Tristram wouldn't continue to receive so much as the quarterly allowance owed him as the second son. Taking away his only means of support was his father's way of punishing him for failing as a military officer.

Not that Tristram considered what he had done a failure. His actions had succeeded quite well and saved dozens of lives. Unfortunately, saving lives was not the outcome the superior officers wanted.

Tristram focused a narrow-eyed glare at his cousin.

"Why did you break that bow and how do you expect to replace it?"

"I'll take the train down to the city and buy a new one." Ambrose stroked the splintered edge of the bow. "It looks rather worn anyway. Miss VanDorn might appreciate something new."

"Purchased with what?" Tristram asked.

Ambrose grinned. "Your largesse, cousin."

"Reward money for retrieving the jewels." Florian made the suggestion without a hint of humor.

"If she hasn't had them all copied and sold the originals." Tristram retrieved the undamaged comb from his coat pocket and held the jewels up to one of the gas sconces set on the wall.

Light glinted in the diamonds, but then, they were faceted enough that even this poor form of illumination would shimmer off them. He needed sunlight and a magnifying glass to be certain these jewels were artificial.

"The ones you found on the continent were real. Or at least the jewelers and pawnbrokers thought so." Florian picked up the cello. "We know she must have sold those."

"But they could have been copied first," Ambrose suggested. "We'd best hurry if we wish to dance with Miss VanDorn again. She may leave at any moment, and we don't have permission to call."

Florian rose, but Tristram blocked the doorway. "Our hostess can leave cards for us."

"If the elder Mrs. Selkirk is willing to do so," Florian said, but Tristram didn't move from the door. "I have the impression that the Selkirks and the VanDorns are not in the habit of making social calls."

"Then we should have made better arrangements." Ambrose joined Florian. "Are you going to get out of our way, cousin?"

"In a moment." Tristram dropped his gaze to the bow. "You still haven't told me why you broke that."

Ambrose's mouth tightened at the corners, forming furrows beside his lips that added ten years to his five and twenty. "Rage. Pure and simple rage that she would steal and lie and cheat her husband, my old friend, and then the Baston-Wards, and act as though she were the affronted one."

"She is rather cool for a lady we accused of stealing a fortune in gemstones." Florian drummed his fingertips on the top of the cello's case.

Tristram recalled seeing her ladyship drumming her fingers against her own wrist and shook his head. "Not as cool as all that. She's anxious about something."

"Being caught in her larceny." Florian grinned as though the prospect of catching her ladyship in the act of thievery pleased him. "Now, if you will excuse us, Tris, we would like to do some pursuing of our own."

Tristram stepped aside and opened the door for the men. They moved down the hall with strides long and fast enough to fall minutely shy of a trot. He followed at a more leisurely pace, getting trapped behind a crowd of older men who reeked of cigar smoke and talked too loudly. They reminded him of his father—wealthy, self-satisfied men who spoke of nothing but stock investments, railroads and land. They talked of ordering this person to do this and that person to do that. How many of those minions were their sons, whom they called disappointments? If any of those sons of these American equivalents of noblemen wanted to go into the church, they, too, would more than likely be shoved into a profession for which they were wholly unsuited, or worse, be like his brother and have no profession at all, to their own destruction.

Perhaps he was being judgmental without cause and many of these men and their offspring wanted to do good in the world, as did Tristram. With the stipend his father promised him if he succeeded in finding the gemstones and proving he was not a ne'er-do-well embarrassment to the Wolfe family, Tristram could continue the charity to help discharged soldiers too damaged by war to take up their old jobs. If he didn't solve the matter of the jewels, his father would remove the income and too many of these forgotten servants of the Crown would die in poverty along with their families.

The steps before him cleared, and he took them down two at a time. He wanted to observe Lady Catherine Bisterne before she was aware of his presence in the ballroom and see if she was as nervous without him around as she had been with him close at hand. He wished to take her hands in his and feel for himself if they were cold with composure or warm with her shame...or the fire he had seen in her luminous dark eyes.

Chapter 3

Paying visits differs from leaving cards in that you must ask to be received.

Emily Price Post

"I told Mr. Wolfe and Mr. Baston-Ward they may call on me today." Estelle's cocoa-brown eyes sparked with golden light behind their fringe of long lashes. "And not for Mama's at home."

Catherine set down the slice of dry toast she had barely touched and stared at her younger sister across the breakfast table. "You can't do that, Stell. They are penniless ne'er-do-wells who are only interested in your trust fund."

"They are interested in my music." Estelle clipped each word. "Both are accomplished musicians who have no instruments on which to practice here."

"They don't even have titles to recommend them."

Color bloomed along Estelle's cheekbones. "I'd rather my friends have only their musical ability to recommend them than someone like your husband, who had only his title to recommend him."

The toast crumbled between Catherine's fingers. Tears stung her eyes and she looked away from Estelle, focusing on the expanse of Tuxedo Lake, white edging the wavelets in the center. A sheen of ice rimmed the shore like her heart—cold on the outside, turbulent in the center.

"You're right, Stell." Catherine's throat constricted so she couldn't speak above a murmur. "Edwin chose to give nothing to the world but his title, but then, that was all I thought I wanted. Well, his title and his handsome face. Which is precisely why I wish to spare you from looking only to the surface of the man."

"I know seeing those men must be difficult for you." Estelle reached across the table and covered Catherine's hand with hers. "But I feel like their presence here is such a godsend. So few people here are accomplished musicians, and Mama never lets me associate with the townspeople anymore."

"I understand they were giving you notions of joining a band." Catherine grimaced, the mere word denoting lower Manhattan factory workers who turned amateur performers on their off days.

"Amy Beach performed in public." Estelle never failed to point out the talented Boston musician and composer as an example of a woman of good family who performed. "With an orchestra. And now she is married and not publicly performing."

Estelle sighed.

"I know you want to play for others, Stell, but playing in a low theater is no life for a VanDorn."

"And what is a life for a VanDorn?" Estelle removed her hand and drummed her long fingers on the lace table runner. "A marriage where my husband stays in the city more nights than he's at home with me and the children? Do you know how pathetic Mrs. Post is, driving down to the train station night after night, hoping her husband will appear? He scarcely does. I'm mortified for her. And then you were stranded in that mausoleum of a house on Romney Marsh while your husband gambled away your dowry in London."

"Bisterne is a very beautiful manor house, not a mausoleum."

"After your money stopped it from crumbling to bits."

"What do you know of it?" Catherine's voice emerged harsher than she intended just as her mother swept into the dining room on a cloud of lavender and rose perfume.

"Girls, you aren't quarreling, are you?"

"No, Mama," they chorused.

"Good. Catherine created quite enough of a stir last night with that mauve-and-green gown, and we don't wish to have the servants gossiping about how the two of you cannot get along with one another." Mama paused in her speech as a footman entered bearing fresh coffee steaming in a silver pot.

He drew out Mama's chair with his free hand, then poured coffee into the cup already set at her place. Mama took only black coffee for breakfast, which was probably why she remained girlishly slim despite her forty-five years. The footman departed the room without so much as offering to fill a plate for her.

"You should have remained for the entire ball," Mama continued. "You looked ashamed of yourself, Catherine. And, Estelle, you will never find a husband if you don't allow young men to court you."

"I don't want—"

Catherine shot her a glance, then faced Mama. "I had developed a headache."

"I saw old Mrs. Selkirk talking to you." Mama raised her coffee to drink and her eyebrows to query.

Catherine raised her own cup as though she and her mother were saluting one another with foils before a duel—coffee cups at five paces. "I'm to stay away from Lord Tristram Wolfe."

Estelle smirked. "Which you didn't."

"He wouldn't stay away from me. In fact—" Catherine took a deep breath. She may as well get this out of the way now. "He's calling this morning."

"Indeed?" Though they were as dark as her daughters', Mama's eyes gleamed from beneath half-mast lids. "Will I be the first mama in Tuxedo Park—or Newport, for that matter—to see her daughter marry two English titles?"

"I have no intention of marrying another Englishman." Catherine pushed back her chair. "And if you want the best for your younger daughter, you will be cautious about allowing Mr. Wolfe and Mr. Baston-Ward to call upon her. They are highly unlikely to inherit titles without a number of men dying prematurely."

As her husband had—far too prematurely—a month short of his thirty-fifth birthday. Edwin had simply never awakened after a night of excesses in dining, drinking and gaming.

"I'm not interested in them as beaux." Estelle rose, plate in hand, and headed for the sideboard. "I wish for someone willing to indulge my love of playing good music. We will practice for an hour this morning."

Unwise of you, little sister. Catherine froze on the edge of her chair, expecting Mama to forbid such a plan.

But Mama's face took on a beatific glow. "Those two nice young men you danced with last night? That sounds a perfectly acceptable form of activity."

"But, Mama, they're—"

"Gentlemen," Mama said, interrupting Catherine's protest. "And where would you like to meet your young man, Catherine?"

Catherine clamped her teeth together to hold back a sharp retort about Tristram not being her young man. Pointing that out would only open up a discussion over why else he would call upon her. Mama did not need to know about his accusations.

"The conservatory." Her jaw was still rigid. This time of year, the room would be freezing with all of that glass. That might convince Tristram to make his stay as brief as possible. "I believe his call is purely business," she added. "At least I hope that's all it is. I truly do not wish to upset Mrs. Selkirk. She believes Georgette has set her sights on Lord Tristram Wolfe."

Mama sighed. "She threatened to ruin us, I suppose?"

"Something like that."

"She hasn't managed to do so yet." Estelle returned to the table with enough ham and eggs on her plate to ensure her girlish figure would soon abandon her. "Or not entirely."

Catherine stiffened. "What do you mean?"

"Nothing important." Estelle took a dainty bite of ham and began to chew with extensive vigor.

Mama sighed. "Estelle was uninvited to a party or two after Mrs. Selkirk learned she had been in the village playing her music with some of the workers."

"I didn't want to go to the parties anyway. Well, not all of them."

"One was a garden party with Mrs. Lorillard, the younger one." Mama blinked as though fighting tears.

Catherine shot to her feet. "I will send a note to Lord Tristram right now telling him not to come. Even if his business is with Bisterne's estate, I won't risk anything else happening to the family."

She stalked from the room and headed for the library.

A freshly filled fountain pen lay on the top of the desk along with a stack of paper and envelopes. She seated herself in the wide leather chair and picked up the pen just as the clock on the mantel chimed eleven.

Of course. The hour was late. Despite leaving the ball early, Catherine hadn't slept until well after Estelle ceased playing the piano and their parents and brother returned from the ball. The clock's four chimes had risen through the floorboards before Catherine slept and she woke six hours later. How Papa and Paul managed to remain at entertainments until past midnight, then catch a train into New York in the morning, she never understood.

She hurried with her note so a footman could carry it over to the Selkirk house on the Wee Wah Pond. Clearheaded in the cold light of day without old Mrs. Selkirk's lingering hostility, she of course remembered she could refuse a call from Lord Tristram Wolfe. Catherine, Lady Bisterne, didn't need to receive a man who outright accused her of a crime.

The quarter hour chimed. There was no time to get across the park to the other lake before Lord Tristram left.

Catherine crumpled the note and tossed it onto the embers of a banked fire. It smoldered on the coals for a moment, flared in a short-lived burst of flame, then died like her brief notion that she could refuse to meet with the younger son of the Marquess of Cothbridge. If she did not, he might tell the Selkirks that he suspected her of being a thief. He might go as far as to contact local authorities or, worse, some diplomatic service between England and America. The resulting scandal would destroy Catherine and her family, despite her innocence.

It was a large step from stealing fiancés to stealing family heirlooms, yet Catherine's detractors would make that leap. She had come home to mend the past, not create more scandals—she must silence Lord Tristram by allaying his suspicions.

She must also keep Estelle from igniting scandal by indulging her music with two gentlemen who were twice removed from inheriting titles—or anything at all.

Catherine, the Dowager Countess of Bisterne, a thief indeed. She had taken nothing that did not belong to her other than Georgette's fiancé. For that act, she had paid nearly every day of her marriage.

"Stolen jewels indeed." With more vigor than was ladylike, Catherine climbed the flaring staircase to her bedchamber. Giving her maid a nod of greeting, she crossed the pink rose-patterned carpet to the window and looked at the lake. The waves frothed like her insides. She should have eaten. She should have thought to send the man packing earlier. She should have…

Too many should-haves filled her life. But her homecoming was supposed to change all that. And therefore, she would start with Lord Tristram Wolfe.

She turned from the window and moved to her dressing table. Smelling faintly of magnolia with her initials in diamond chips on the lid, her jewel case rested atop the golden wood. The bottom drawer held the other jewels Bisterne had given her during their marriage, pieces he declared were not part of the family set. Considering he had lied about the hair combs, she doubted she could trust his word about these, either. She pulled a string of amber beads out of the box and held them up to the light. Despite the grayness of the day, the beads glowed and warmed in her hand. Artificial amber, if it existed, could not do this. Or could it?

Catherine laid the beads on the dressing tabletop and pulled out a brooch with a ruby surrounded by pearls. "Sapphire?" she called to her lady's maid.

"Yes, my lady?" Sapphire glanced up from the window seat where she perched with a pile of mending on her lap.

"You were a lady's maid for twenty years before you came to work for me, were you not?"

"Twenty-two, yes, my lady." Sapphire's dark gray eyes narrowed. "Is there a problem with the quality of my work?"

"Not at all. I was thinking perhaps you'd know a bit about jewels." Catherine held the ruby toward the light. "Is this real or paste?"

Sapphire's eyes widened. "My Lord Bisterne gave that to you."

Catherine said nothing.

"It's beautiful, my lady, and will look fine against that blue silk you had made up at Worth's in Paris."

Catherine ran her thumbnail across a pearl, wondering if Sapphire would think her stark-staring mad if she tried to bite one of the gemstones to see if it had that gritty feel only true pearls exhibited. "If I dare wear—"

A knock sounded on the door. Catherine jumped and jabbed the pin of the brooch into her thumb. She didn't need to open the door to know a footman stood beyond it to tell her Lord Tristram had arrived.

While she wrapped her bleeding thumb in a handkerchief, Sapphire answered the door. Lord Tristram had indeed arrived on the stroke of eleven-thirty. Catherine nodded assent that she would receive him and unwrapped her thumb. Only a few drops of blood marred the whiteness of the black-bordered linen, but the digit throbbed too much for gloves to be comfortable.

"It's morning. It's my parents' home. I won't look improperly dressed without gloves." She spoke the excuses aloud as she patted a stray tendril of hair back into place before the mirror.

The reflection of her diamond engagement ring and wedding band winked back at her. She dropped her hand and stared at the diamond-crusted circlets. The rings were Baston-Ward heirlooms—her husband had made that clear on their wedding day. Catherine had not removed them from her hand once in five years. Going into muted colors after only a year and a month was one way to announce her widowhood, but removing the engagement ring and wedding ring band was quite another statement, a declaration that she would accept advances from other gentlemen, which she would not.

Yet how could she walk downstairs and declare her innocence to Lord Tristram Wolfe when she did indeed wear jewelry that did not belong to her?

* * *

Tristram walked from the Selkirks' imitation Elizabethan house to the VanDorn home. He hoped the exercise and biting air would ease the tension gripping him. But by the time he climbed the steps to the curving edifice of Lake House, his guts felt as though they had turned into watch springs.

He pressed the doorbell, then stood drumming his fingers against his thighs. A second before the door opened, he remembered to remove a calling card from his pocket to hand to the silver-haired butler.

"'Lord Tristram Wolfe.'" The man read from the card. "Her ladyship is expecting you."

Tristram followed the man's straight back across a corridor that curved gently away from the door. Several rooms opened along the hall's length, and he expected the butler to show him into one of these—a parlor, the library, even a cozy sitting room perhaps. Instead, the man headed up the staircase, pausing where it widened into a landing.

"Make yourself comfortable, my lord. Lady Bisterne will be with you shortly." The butler bowed and withdrew.

Tristram stared at the panorama before him. The chamber stood out from the house to allow floor-to-ceiling windows on three sides. The abundance of glass made for a chilly chamber, and a view that made up for the cold—the wind-whipped waters of the lake and the woods beyond; gardens, a gazebo surrounded by spruce trees and the house itself, which curved along the shore.

"Astounding." The word escaped his lips.

"It is, rather."

He startled at the sound of her voice behind him. Half smiling, he faced her ladyship and held out his hand. "Thank you for receiving me, Lady Bisterne."

"Of course." She accepted his proffered hand.

Her fingers felt like icicles against his palm, and for a

moment, he fought the urge to clasp her hand in his and warm it. The action would have given him a moment to gaze at her by the light of day, for she was worth a moment—or a hundred—of gazing.

She'd been pretty by the gaslights of the clubhouse. But here, even in the gray of a day threatening more rain, her complexion glowed like a natural pearl, emphasizing the depth of dark eyes behind lashes long and thick. The dark green jacket and skirt she wore brought out the red in her smooth hair. All of her was smooth, neat perfection except for that dimple in her chin. That dimple, that slip of the sculptor's chisel, served to emphasize the flawlessness of her bones, while making her far more approachable, far more…appealing. Too appealing.

No wonder Bisterne had fallen for her. The wonder was how he had managed to leave her behind at Bisterne, while he cavorted in London.

His mouth suddenly dry, Tristram tucked his thumbs into the pockets of his coat and tore his gaze from Catherine. A suite of sofas and chairs rested upon a Persian carpet in the center of the room. "May we be seated? This may take a while."

"I will send for coffee." Her nostrils pinched. "Or would you prefer tea?"

Perhaps the VanDorns' cook made better tea than did the Selkirks', but her face told him she disliked that oh-so-English beverage. "Coffee is well enough."

While she rang for a footman to bring up coffee, Tristram returned his attention to the lake. The waves had died down and precipitation that suspiciously resembled snow fell lightly like feathers from a pillow. "Snow at the beginning of November."

"Not uncommon here. They've been seeing a bit here and there since the middle of October."

He glanced over his shoulder. Seeing she had seated

herself on a sofa facing the windows, he settled on a chair across from her. "They? You weren't here?"

"I only arrived in Tuxedo Park three days ago."

"Yes, from Dieppe. Wouldn't Le Havre have been more convenient?"

Her hands flattened on the brown velvet cushion, and a stillness settled over her. "How do you know where I was in France?" Her voice was as cold and brittle as the ice rimming the edge of the lake.

"I thought I would—"

The arrival of coffee, hot and fragrant, along with cream, sugar and sweet biscuits, interrupted him. Her question and his partial response hovered in the air while she thanked the footman, then poured Tristram coffee, adding a dollop of cream and pinch of sugar he preferred. Not until she settled back on the sofa, a fragile china cup cradled in her hands, did he continue.

"I thought I could catch up with you in Paris, and then Le Havre, but I miscalculated your direction there, and arrived in New York a week ahead of you."

Her eyes widened, a little too far for genuine surprise, as far as Tristram was concerned. "Why, may I ask, were you following me?"

"To recover the jewels, of course." He smiled.

She gave him a blank stare, sipped her coffee, then set the cup on the low table between them. Light from the wall sconces flashed off the diamond-studded wedding band and matching engagement ring on her left hand, rings that should grace the far less attractive fingers of the current Countess of Bisterne, Florian's sister-in-law.

Tristram leaned forward and slipped his hand beneath Lady Catherine Bisterne's, tilting it so a cold flame burned at the heart of the engagement diamond, and asked, "Shall we start with these rings?"

Chapter 4

Blood drained from Catherine's face. Beneath Tristram's grip, the rings warmed. Her eyes squeezed shut, and her lips, no longer dusky rose, compressed.

"Please." Her voice rasped barely above a whisper, and she tugged her hand free.

Tristram considered rising and crossing the room so he could bang his head against one of the myriad glass panes in the windows to knock some sense into himself. She hadn't just been reacting in guilt; he had been holding her hand too tightly.

"I am sorry, my lady." An urge to raise her hand to his lips washed over him. If blood had drained from her face, then it surely flooded into his, for his ears and cheeks burned. His necktie grew too tight. "I forgot myself."

"I'd ask you to leave but I believe we have unfinished business." Her hands steady, her expression now the smooth mask adopted by a lady used to court circles, she refilled both their cups. Instead of picking up hers, she twisted off the rings and laid them on the table, where the diamonds winked and shimmered like lighthouse beacons warning of danger ahead. "As you can see, I have never taken them off." Her ring finger bore the marks of rings long worn. "I was afraid to remove them lest people think I was hunting for another husband." Two rapid blinks betrayed emotion trying to break through her facade. "I'd recommend you tell old Mrs. Selkirk that, but then you would have to admit you were here."

"I expect she already knows." He seized on the diversion like a man stuck in quicksand grasping a rope to haul himself out. "I had to ask the Selkirks' butler for directions."

"They wouldn't lend you their carriage?"

"I wanted to walk."

This time, the widening of her eyes appeared to be natural surprise. "You wanted to walk in this cold?"

She glanced at the windows. Beyond the glass, snow swirled like confetti defying gravity, never touching the ground. What flakes did land melted on impact, leaving the winter-brown grass and walkways to the gazebo and lake wet.

"After two years in South Africa," Tristram said, "I appreciate precipitation regardless of the temperature."

"You were in South Africa?" She gave him a look of sincere interest.

He returned it with a rueful shrug. "Not a shining hour of mine. The Boer War."

"I remember hearing something about you being in the

military. You—" She pressed her fingers to her lips as though trying to shove back the rest of her thought.

He bowed his head. "Captain Lord Tristram Wolfe at your service, my lady."

Except he didn't have a true right to use the military rank. He hoped she didn't recall that bit of gossip that must have made its way to Bisterne. He had, after all, been allowed to resign his commission.

"But since I resigned," he hastened to emphasize this fact, "I never use the rank."

"You were wounded." Her glance flicked to his head. "Are you certain you're quite well?"

His hand flew to flatten his cowlick, and he narrowed his eyes at her. "Are you suggesting that my conviction that you are responsible for the missing Bisterne jewels is a result of my being bashed on the head?"

"I would never be so vulgar."

"You're wearing colors. The vulgarity of that was all Mrs. Selkirk talked of at breakfast this morning."

Catherine laughed.

At the sound of her laughter, an invisible hand wound the already taut watch springs of Tristram's middle, causing friction, too much warmth. He drank his now cold coffee in an attempt to ease the tension inside him.

"Shall I order fresh coffee so we may start this conversation over, Lord Tristram?" Catherine rose without waiting for his response, and crossed the room to the bell. "My sister tells me she is trying to convince our father that an internal telephone system will save the servants a great deal of work running up and down steps, as we could call them with our request."

Tristram raised his brows at this sudden chatter. It, like the way she stabbed the bell push three times instead of one, spoke as loudly as her voice of her nervousness.

"But then," Catherine continued, "Estelle likes gadgets.

She is forever recording her own music on her phonograph cylinders. I prefer to listen to live music myself, and perhaps one day—"

The arrival of the footman stopped the uninterrupted string of words—a string suggesting nervousness on her part, or an effort to keep him from saying anything to her. She gave the order for fresh coffee, remaining silent until the footman removed the tray of used cups, his stare fixed on the discarded rings.

The instant the man's footfalls no longer sounded on the stair treads, Tristram rather expected her ladyship to take up her flow of chatter where she had left off. Instead, she glided across the room to a set of windows, her soft wool skirt flowing around her like dark green water.

"Enough fencing, my Lord Tristram." She spoke with her back to him, though the day had grown so dark with cloud cover her reflection shone in the glass. "Tell me what transformed you from soldier to Scotland Yard detective? Tell me why you and my cousin by marriage have accused me of stealing jewels from the Bisterne estate. Other than the wedding and engagement ring, of course. I never thought about how they belonged to the estate until this morning, before your call. Surely you didn't chase me across Europe because of a couple of paltry rings."

Paltry? The new Earl of Bisterne could feed every tenant on his estate for a year with the price of those rings alone.

Tristram said nothing for a full minute, then he rose and joined her at the window. "I'm scarcely a Scotland Yard detective, my lady. We have a family connection to the current Lord Bisterne, and his father was a friend of my father's from the time they were in short pants until Baston-Ward's death a half dozen years ago. Baston-Ward had made some foolish investments that ruined his fortune, and his son tried to recoup those losses through gaming instead of hard work."

"A trait of the family," Catherine murmured.

Tristram inclined his head in acknowledgment. "Which is why the estate fell into such disrepair."

"It isn't in disrepair now, thanks to my dowry." A hint of bitterness edged her tone.

Tristram barely managed to stop himself from reaching out and touching her hand, her elbow, her face in a gesture of comfort. She had made her bed. If Edwin had not been such a profligate in gaming, drink and food consumption, she would still be lying in that bed of neglect after buying her way into the English nobility. Surely she had known the risks, but then, perhaps she had not. She couldn't have been above eighteen or nineteen years of age when she succumbed to the lure of a title and Bisterne's charm.

"You gave a number of people much-needed work." He offered truth for comfort instead of his touch.

"But that won't last. The dowry reverted back to my trust fund principle upon my husband's death."

"Which is where the jewels come in. Bisterne needs to sell them to gain capital enough to continue the estate into a paying prospect."

The footman returned with the chime of silver and the rattle of china. Out the window, the snow had turned to freezing rain that pattered against the glass. When the footman departed, the soaring notes of a violin rose in his wake.

"That's not Ambrose playing, is it?"

"That is Estelle. We don't know where she gets her talent. Mama and even my father and brother can play adequately at the piano, but Estelle's talent is special."

"I hear that."

Estelle was playing Vivaldi with a warmth that probably would have pleased the composer. It pleased Tristram, cutting straight to his heart as good music should. With those glorious notes swooping up the staircase, discussing

Lady Catherine's larceny seemed as much a crime as taking someone else's jewelry.

"My lady." His throat felt tight. "I didn't believe my father when he told me the Bisterne jewels were missing and you were the only person who could have taken them. But I set out to follow you anyway, and found too much evidence to deny the charge."

"You are referring to more than the wedding and engagement rings." Her voice was expressionless, but he could not see her face.

"Considerably more." He was growing numb standing so close to the expanse of glass. "Shall we sit?" He could see her better if they faced one another across a coffee service rather than staring into the autumnal gloom side by side.

Wordlessly, she returned to the sofa, touched her fingertips to the side of the coffeepot and poured them fresh cups. Neither of them drank. They sat in identical poses, their backs too straight to touch the cushions behind them, their gazes fixed somewhere beyond the other's shoulders.

Then Catherine blinked twice and met his eyes in a challenge. "So what is this evidence?"

"You spent the past thirteen months in Italy and France." He drew up a mental list. "Venice, Rome and Florence. Avignon, Lyon and Paris. In each of those cities, at a jeweler, I found at least one piece of jewelry that I know for a fact had previously been in your possession."

A lifetime of training kept Catherine's face expressionless, her teeth clenched together. If she opened her mouth for so much as a sip of coffee, she would probably shriek with hysterical laughter or say something unforgivably rude to Tristram.

He shifted on his chair, set down his cup and drew a sheaf of papers from an inside pocket of his coat. "Receipts." He held them out to her. "For the pieces I managed to recover."

She snatched the receipts from him and scanned prices in lira and francs. Each bill of purchase was attached to a detailed description and drawing.

"Who made these?" She tapped on the pictures.

"They were in the vault where the jewels should have been."

"I never saw them there."

"So you did go into the vault?"

She slapped the papers onto the sofa beside her. "Of course I did. I was mistress of the house. We kept coin there for paying workmen and wages on quarter days. Bisterne was rarely at home, so that duty fell to me. I never even saw most of the jewelry. Other than a parure of emeralds, I never wore any of it. It wasn't to my taste."

"And the combs?"

"Those were a wedding gift." To her horror, tears filled her eyes. She blinked, but to no avail. "And you know they are artificial. Perhaps they all are."

Tristram shifted on his chair. Finally, he produced a white linen handkerchief and pressed it into her hand. "None of them, according to the jewelers, are artificial. And in thirteen months, you had plenty of time to have copies made."

"I wouldn't wear paste gemstones." She dashed the handkerchief across her eyes, then crushed it between her fingers. "I think you need to leave, my lord. You have been here long enough, and my intentions are to make amends with Georgette Selkirk, not make matters worse between our families." She rose to force him to do so.

He was too well-bred not to, but he gave her an uncompromising stare. "No one else had access to the jewels except for you and Edwin. But Edwin was already gone, so that leaves you. I *will* find a way to prove you have, or know where to find, the rest."

"You may try, my lord, but you are forgetting one important detail."

"Indeed?"

"Why would I do such a thing? My quarterly allowance from my trust fund holds more money than all the Bisterne jewels put together."

For a heartbeat, his eyes flickered with uncertainty. Then he smiled and bowed. "Touché, my lady. I will find my motivation."

"You are welcome to try, Mr. Holmes."

He laughed at her reference to Sir Arthur Conan Doyle's famous detective. "I will find a reason, my lady. I likely have more of a stake in winning this game than do you." He executed the most fluid and graceful bow she had witnessed since her husband's death, then clasped her hand in his and raised her fingers to his lips.

A jolt of electricity shot through her, and she snatched her hand away. "How dare you?" The whispered words lacked the hauteur she wished for.

"With very little trouble." He smiled, turned so smartly on his heels she expected him to salute the portrait of her grandfather hanging at the top of the steps, then strode from the room.

Once he descended the steps, Catherine sank onto the sofa. She started to cover her face with her hands until she regained her composure—and spotted the rings still lying on the table.

So he was not as confident as he pretended. He wouldn't have forgotten the rings if he were.

"He can do without them."

Yet it was legitimately within his milieu to take them from her on behalf of the new Lord Bisterne. They never should have left England on her finger. She could have purchased a plain gold band to let the world know she was not in the market for a second spouse.

She would catch him up and give him the rings. He would not find in her more reasons to accuse her of being a jewel thief.

She snatched up the band and betrothal diamond and raced down the steps to the entryway. It stood stark and empty, cold stone lighted by long windows on either side of the front door.

She flung open that door and gazed down the path leading through the trees to the road. Swirling snow stuck to the grass and flagstones, descending now in sheets instead of dancing through the air. If Lord Tristram were out there, she could not see him. If she tried to follow, she would likely slip and fall in her light leather shoes, not to mention freeze in her thin wool jacket and lace-trimmed shirtwaist.

Already shivering, she shut the door, headed for the nearest fire and heard the music recommence. It was a cello this time, an instrument Estelle hadn't mastered as well as she liked.

The cellist playing, however, had mastered it.

"Florian." Catherine sprinted for the music room door as though the corridor were a tennis court and she needed to get to the ball.

She yanked open the door. The music stuttered to a halt. Estelle spun around on the piano stool to glare at Catherine. And three gentlemen stood, two with instruments and bows in hand. The third held nothing but a top hat.

No wonder Lord Tristram had managed to disappear so quickly. He hadn't left the house at all.

She closed the door and leaned against it to support her suddenly wobbly legs.

"Don't tell us to stop." Estelle widened her eyes in entreaty. "This piece was just coming together."

"Your sister is a wonderful composer, Lady Bisterne."
Florian gave Estelle a look of pure devotion.

"Estelle, a composer?" Catherine shook her head. She
raised her hand to rub the taut muscles in her neck and remembered the rings she still clutched. "I'd like to hear it."

"We were just about to play it for Lord Tristram." Estelle faced the piano and rested her hands on the keyboard.
"I call this 'Praise.'"

Praise, indeed. For the next ten minutes, the music rose
to the heavens, a beautiful reminder that Catherine had
spent too little time in praise over the past five years. Or
perhaps in her life. Though far from perfect, with the men
having just learned the piece, the instruments delivered the
tune into her heart.

When the last note vanished from the room, the five
of them remained silent, everyone seeming to hold his or
her breath.

The chime of the doorbell broke the stillness. The three
musicians exchanged smiles of congratulations. On the far
side of the room, Lord Tristram bowed to Estelle. "A reminder of what so rarely falls from our lips."

"If we had a poet who could write lyrics…" Florian
began.

"And a voice capable of singing them…" Ambrose
added.

"We could make a fortune singing this for—"

"Do not," Catherine growled, "encourage her. One scandal in the family is more than enough."

And there it was—a reminder of her elopement with
Edwin and the missing jewels. Exactly what Lord Tristram did not need.

To distract them all, Catherine rested her hand on Estelle's shoulder. "I'll make a bargain with you, baby sister. If you promise to attend all the social events Mama

wishes you to attend, I will see to it you may practice as much as you like."

"With Mr. Wolfe and Mr. Baston-Ward?" Estelle looked up with shining eyes. "Truly?"

"Yes, truly. But do, please, for propriety's sake, ask Sapphire or one of the other maids to join you in the future." Catherine squeezed the delicate bones beneath her hand. "A deal?"

"A deal." Estelle shot to her feet and enveloped Catherine in an embrace. "I don't care what anyone says about you. You always were the best sister a girl could have."

"Wait until the holiday season of parties is over before you make those kinds of declarations." Her tone was stern, but her heart swelled.

Then Lord Tristram strode up to them, and the rings seemed to catch fire inside her fist. Slowly, painfully, she forced her fingers open and held out her hand, the rings gleaming in the snowy light. "You forgot these."

"Thank you." He removed the rings from her palm without touching her."

Catherine lifted her chin. "To be frank, I'm happy you're taking away my last reminder of a man—I do apologize, Florian, but the truth here is necessary—for whom I was a good and faithful wife, though he broke nearly every one of our vows. I no longer want a reminder of my greatest mistake."

"Thank you for saying so, my lady." Tristram tucked the rings into his pocket and pinned her with a stare so intense she nearly had to look away. "And for giving me a missing piece in this puzzle."

Chapter 5

Motivation. She had given him a motivation for stealing the Bisterne jewels—revenge. Catherine read it in the satisfaction on his face.

A dozen protests of her innocence rose to her lips, but she suppressed them all. When she was an adolescent roaming a little too freely around the newly developed Tuxedo Park, and denied getting up to mischief with her friends, Papa reminded her that one could not prove a negative unless she possessed a good alibi.

In this event, she possessed no alibi. Nor could she prove the negative, that she had not taken the jewels. She had to find a way to prove her innocence.

Or the guilt of someone else.

"Believe what you like, my lord. I will prove you wrong." She returned his direct, challenging glare.

Sparks crackled between them and she felt a jolt of power as though she were an incandescent light.

He stepped back as though he felt it, too. "I should be going. The Selkirks are expecting me for luncheon." A huskiness roughened the clarity of his oh-so-English voice.

"Do stay, my lord, all of you." Estelle rose from the piano stool. "I will tell the cook to expect three more."

"Thank you, no." Tristram headed for the door.

"I will send for the carriage." Catherine hastened to beat Estelle to the bell. "The auto will never be able to drive in this snow."

"Neither is necessary, Lady Bisterne." Tristram yanked open the door, stepped over the threshold and was gone, not awaiting the butler to show him out.

"He must have forgotten his manners in Cape Town." Florian touched his bow to the cello strings. "Do we have time to play a bit more before luncheon?"

Ambrose set aside his violin and picked up Estelle's banjo. "Will you show us how this works, Miss VanDorn?"

"The banjo? It's a lady's instrument, at least it is here. I believe in the South, the men play it. But if you like..." Estelle swept across the room, skirt flaring with the speed of her movement, and took possession of the banjo.

Catherine left them to it. Finding a maid replenishing the fire in the dining room, she asked her to first tell the cook two gentlemen would be joining them for luncheon, and then to sit as chaperone in the music room. Then Catherine climbed the steps to her mother's boudoir.

She found her parent seated at her desk with a pile of invitations she was addressing and a frown furrowing her brow. "What do you think of this new fashion of ringing people up to invite them to dinner?"

"I think it lacks elegance." Catherine breathed in the familiar and comforting scent of lavender and roses.

Mama began to address one more envelope. "But this is so tedious. If I used our telephone, I could have Sims do all the calling."

Catherine smiled at the notion of their aging butler calling each prospective guest as though bestowing a great favor upon them.

Mama consulted her list. "This is a smallish dinner party, rather informal. More an excuse for us ladies to gather discreetly and discuss the annual Christmas tea, while the men talk politics."

"That's a lovely idea." Catherine settled herself on a lavender-and-cream-striped sofa. "May I assist you?"

"I would like nothing better, but surely you have friends to call on or shopping excursions in the city to arrange?"

Catherine looked down at her hands folded in her lap, covering her denuded left hand with her right. "I did more than enough shopping in France and Italy to last another year or two. And as for friends…" Her throat closed. "I rather scuttled those relationships when I eloped with Georgette's fiancé."

Mama sighed and returned her pen to its holder. "That was five years ago. It's past time everyone forgot about your youthful folly. See, you've already had a gentleman caller. Did you have a pleasant coze?"

"Lord Tristram is as warm as the conservatory without a fire. I am still to blame for my disastrous marriage."

"Hmph." Mama brought her fist down on her desk. "And what about Lord Bisterne's behavior? He made a promise to her and broke it. Why does everyone blame you as though you forced him to the altar?"

Catherine's heart warmed at Mama's never-failing loyalty. "I did flirt with him outrageously. You told me to stop."

"And if he truly cared for Georgette, no amount of flirtation would have swayed him to run off with you."

"My greater dowry persuaded him."

"Estelle is about to follow in your footsteps if we're not careful."

"I thought she'd have learned her lesson with me for an example, but you are so right, Mama, in more ways than one."

"Those young men in the music room are fortune hunters, as well?"

"Without the dubious honor of bearing a title."

"Neither of these young men have either money or title prospects?"

"Neither. But if I may offer you some advice from my own experience, don't deny her access to them. I believe now that if I had been allowed to spend more time in Bisterne's company, I would have learned his pious talk and fine manners covered an empty soul."

Mama sifted through the stack of engraved invitations. "I will discuss your suggestion with your father tonight. We don't like this notion Estelle has of joining a band, of all things. As if a girl of good birth would ever do such a thing. I'm happy enough to have her perform here, but in public? Out of the question."

"And yet her talent is special."

"It is." Mama's face glowed, smooth and lovely in the lamplight. "We pray her faith will anchor her in doing the right thing with her music."

"Did you hope my faith would persuade me to make the right choices?"

"I'm afraid we did, but worldliness got ahold of you." Mama leaned forward and covered Catherine's clasped hands with one of hers.

Catherine avoided meeting Mama's eyes. "I need to find forgiveness here, but Mrs. Selkirk says I will not be received and Georgette will not speak with me."

"Then Georgette will be in the wrong, not you. As long as you conduct yourself with impeccable behavior and we can keep Estelle from running off, your being home can finally set that old scandal of yours behind us, where it belongs."

Catherine flinched away from Mama's kindly meant words. If she could not prove her innocence to Lord Tristram, a new scandal could damage her family right to its core. Estelle would be the sister of a jewel thief and would never find a decent man to marry her, and other men might refuse to do business with Papa and Paul, thus ruining the family financially. A family that had given her so much in love, forgiveness and money all her life deserved better than that.

Whatever course of action was necessary, she would take it to protect her family.

Tristram needed the walk through the biting cold to calm him before he felt ready for a civilized meal with the Selkirks. Never in his life had a female set his blood to boiling as did Lady Catherine Bisterne. She may as well have been holding a rapier in salute before an old-fashioned duel with that last glance of hers. American-born or not, she could have given any duchess a run for her money in the hauteur division.

Suddenly, he laughed, his voice ringing out along the empty road lined with trees that hid the opulent houses beyond. She might have been nervous around him last night, but today she had herself well in hand, and the result was...

Alarmingly charming.

Tristram shoved his hands into the pockets of his coat and felt the rings she had given him. As he paced up the hill to the Selkirk cottage, he held the wedding band between forefinger and thumb. It was a heavy band for fingers as slender as Catherine's. The diamonds weren't set into channels, but rose over the edges of the band in a way that must have abraded her other fingers. Not a comfortable ring to wear for five years, and yet she hadn't removed it, though she could have exchanged it for a plain gold band without receiving any censure. She had taken these valuable rings from the estate by her own admission—she was the only person at Bisterne with access to the safe at the time of her husband's death, and he had found pieces of the missing jewelry in her wake across Europe. In short, he held three powerful pieces of evidence.

But figuring out a motive was even more precious.

Yet if she *were* guilty, would she not hand over the rest of the jewels before the truth emerged and created a scandal? The strength of her protestations of innocence pointed to her telling the truth. According to old Lady Selkirk, Catherine's elopement five years earlier had created such a scandal, a handful of families, including the Selkirks, avoided the VanDorns whenever possible. Now, with Estelle to launch into society, another scandal could damage her chances of making a good match. Worse, the revelation that Catherine was not the kind and trustworthy lady her family thought she was would damage—even ruin—the affection he had witnessed between the sisters.

His conscience pricked him, and he paused to gaze back down the hill toward the VanDorns' beautiful Lake House. Just the chimneys showed above the trees. He smelled the smoke from the fires, sharp and tangy, in the brisk air. Hearth and home, a family that seemed to care about one another, unlike his...and he could tear it apart.

"Yet what choice do I have?"

If only the fortunes of the Baston-Wards mattered in this pursuit, Tristram wouldn't care so much—they were already nearly penniless due to their own mismanagement and poor behavior. But many others not at fault would suffer if the family could not restore their fortune. They employed dozens of people on the estate and most of them would lose their jobs. If they weren't working, tradesmen in the village would make less money supplying them with their needs. They in turn would be able to buy less.... And so began the destruction of a parish. Similar events had taken place all over England and the continent, as those with land lived beyond their means, made bad investments and gambled away once great fortunes. Money from American heiresses had saved many an estate as well as the jobs of the local people. Catherine's money had made improvements at Bisterne, but it had departed with her, and now the jewels were all the family possessed.

"She needs to return the money she received for the jewels she sold, and return the rest." His frustration burst forth in words spoken aloud to the last snowflakes still drifting to the ground, then he looked up and addressed the Lord. "What else can I do but make her admit the truth?"

Silence met him, broken only by a birdcall he didn't recognize. There'd been silence when he cried out to the Lord for guidance ever since he listened to his heart and found himself on the brink of facing a court-martial for disobeying orders—orders that would have seen dozens of innocent people killed. He would face that court-martial again if he had to, and make the same decision. This situation, however, presented him with choices that would improve his life while helping others, and that self-interest blurred the lines between right and wrong.

Growing cold standing still, Tristram recommenced his climb to the Selkirk house. Georgette and Pierce expected him to be at luncheon. They wanted to discuss some activity or other they were planning, a day trip into New York. Perhaps he could spend an extra day and visit the finer jewelers to see what he could turn up. Meanwhile, Georgette and Pierce were comfortable companions, even if Pierce and his grandmother made clear that they would like a match between Tristram and Georgette.

The idea had crossed Tristram's mind once or twice since he'd met the pretty and gentle-spirited Georgette. An American heiress would solve a number of problems for Tristram.

If only looking into her sky-blue eyes made him feel

as though he were standing at the foot of an oak during a thunderstorm.

When he arrived, the butler led him into the dining room, where luncheon was already underway.

"I do apologize for my tardiness." He seated himself at the last place setting. "I tarried along the road."

"Couldn't they be bothered to send a carriage with you?" The older Mrs. Selkirk set her water glass on the table with a thud. "They have no manners for being among the first families of New York. Georgette is much more refined than the VanDorn daughters, and she is only the second generation of heiresses."

Blushing, Georgette passed a basket of rolls to Tristram. "We'll have hot soup for you momentarily. You look half-frozen."

"They did offer me transport, but I like the cold and chose to walk." Tristram smiled at her, and she blushed more deeply.

"Don't know why you had to go down to Lake House as it is," Mrs. Selkirk continued.

"And nor do you need to." Georgette's mother, a faded version of her daughter, spoke from the far end of the table. "If he had business with Lady Bisterne, then he had business with her and it's none of our business."

"Are you still free this afternoon?" Pierce asked.

"Catherine always was a wild one." The eldest lady scooped butter onto a bite of roll. "And the younger one is following in her footsteps. How they managed to produce such a quiet and steady son is beyond my comprehension. Paul works hard in the city every day." She fixed her gaze on Pierce. "Unlike some young men I know."

Pierce laughed as a footman with a bowl of steaming soup entered and set the bowl before Tristram. Aromas of leeks and creamy chicken stock reminded him he hadn't eaten for hours and had taken two walks in the cold. If he weren't careful, he might gobble down the food like a barbarian.

"Paul VanDorn," Pierce said once the footman departed with empty plates, "is dull."

"I think he's very nice." Georgette spoke to her empty plate.

"And handsome," her mother added.

"It's a handsome family." Pierce grinned.

Mrs. Selkirk banged her cane on the floor like a gavel. "Handsome is as handsome does, and they haven't done handsomely yet."

"Perhaps," Georgette's mother said, "Lady Bisterne is a friend of Lord Tristram's and we should watch what we say around him."

"She can't be friends to anyone after what she did to our George—"

"Grandmother, please." Georgette's hands flew to her cheeks, which were once again the color of the peonies in the gardens back at Cothbridge.

Tristram devoted himself to his soup and pretended not to notice.

After the pause for servants to deliver plates of fish and vegetables, Pierce began a discussion of when they should take the train to New York and what they should see there. That got them through the meal without more remarks about the VanDorn family. But Mrs. Selkirk turned her ire on Pierce for not taking the train into the city every day to work with his father.

Pierce, losing his good humor for once, flashed his grandmother an annoyed glance. "I do go into the city every day and work. I even do so on many Saturdays. But right now, I have a visit from a friend I haven't seen in eight years and am taking a holiday."

They agreed to take their dessert in the drawing room, knowing well that the old lady never ate away from a table and would go to her room to nap after the meal. Georgette's mother murmured something about counting linens and left her children and Tristram alone.

"I apologize for Grandmother," Georgette said the instant her mother departed. "She never used to be so bitter."

"Which may be the worst crime Catherine committed." Pierce stretched his legs toward the fire. "Grandmother grew up the daughter of a Pennsylvania coal miner, pretty enough to marry the boss but ended up owning the mine. She has never forgiven how Catherine kept our family from climbing even higher than invitations to Mrs. Astor's annual ball."

"If rumors are true," Georgette said in her honey-sweet voice, "Catherine saved me from a difficult life. Still…" She shook her head. "Enough of that. Would you like to see the Statue of Liberty?"

"I would."

He had caught a glimpse of it as his ship entered the harbor at New York, but he would enjoy seeing the gift from France close-up. For some reason, he pictured Lady Liberty with Catherine's elegant bones and proud—nearly haughty—carriage, and he smiled with more warmth than he should feel at any thought of her ladyship.

They left for New York the next day. Mrs. Selkirk would join them for some shopping, and Ambrose and Florian, coming in late in the afternoon, thought they would also enjoy the tour, as well. They'd stay in the city for three days, residing in the Selkirks' brownstone overlooking Central Park.

New York wasn't London. Nonetheless, Tristram enjoyed the sights and fine restaurants, the entertainments and dancing with Georgette at an impromptu party at the Selkirks' house. The only flaw in the excursion was the discovery of a pearl-and-ruby pendant that matched the description and drawing of one of the Bisterne baubles, sold to a jeweler on Fifth Avenue.

"Surely she wouldn't be so foolish as to sell something in her own back garden," Florian said.

"She was scarcely in town long enough to do so," Ambrose pointed out.

But the proof lay on Tristram's palm, bright and cold, and Catherine's words regarding her unfortunate marriage rang in his ears, dark and cold and full of pain.

"Sometimes, I wonder if I should marry Georgette Selkirk and forget trying to prove that Lady Bisterne is a thief," Tristram said.

Florian choked on his tea. "What about your father? What about your inheritance?"

"Neither would matter if I married an heiress. Perhaps it's the kinder option." Tristram could spare the VanDorns humiliation or worse, and he'd acquire a lovely wife who made no secret of her Christian faith going deeper than church on Sundays with the other fashionables.

He began to contemplate the notion of marriage on the way back to Tuxedo Park. He and Georgette shared a seat and conversed with the ease of long-standing friends. After another month, if this camaraderie continued, he would probably be foolish not to make Georgette an offer.

But something about the idea simply didn't sit right with Tristram, something having nothing to do with Georgette herself. For reasons he couldn't entirely explain, his mind traveled once again to Lady Bisterne, and the jewel he'd found in the city.

One of the footmen knocked on Tristram's bedroom door as he was dressing for dinner that evening. "You have several messages and some mail, sir. I beg your pardon— Lord Wolfe—"

"'Sir' is quite all right." Tristram took the correspondences off the footman's tray. "'Lord' is merely courtesy and holds very little meaning. Thank you."

He took the messages and letters to the desk and sorted through them. Missives from his father he set aside for later, along with two letters from former army friends. He read the handwritten notations from telephone calls—invitations to dinners, a shooting party and a musical evening.

The last message left him standing, lips compressed, until the dinner bell rang.

The caller was Sims, the VanDorns' butler, on behalf of Mrs. VanDorn and had come through a mere quarter hour before the Selkirk party returned from the city. She was terribly sorry to be calling so tardily, but would he be willing to even up her table at a dinner party the following evening? The husband of one of her guests had been called away at the last minute and she didn't wish for his wife to have to cry off, as well.

And there it was, the frisson of energy he experienced when near Lady Bisterne went whipping through him at the mere suggestion he might see her again.

It was a good reason to refuse.

But the pearl-and-ruby pendant tucked into his hand-kerchief drawer was a good reason to say yes.

He settled himself at the desk, drew out stationery and pen, and wrote a note accepting the invitation.

Chapter 6

People always talk to their neighbors at table whether
introduced or not. It would be a breach of etiquette
not to!

Emily Price Post

"You did what, Mama?"

Seated on a sofa in the drawing room, Catherine looked
up from her needlework to stare at her mother with horror.

Estelle glanced up from the music score she was studying. "You could at least have invited Mr. Baston-Ward or
Mr. Wolfe."

"Or someone else altogether." Catherine's stomach performed a few somersaults, not enough, alas, for her to claim
illness and absent herself from the party. If she did, Mama
might be unwise enough to invite Georgette.

Surely Mama wasn't trying to match Catherine with
another Englishman. The very idea sent her stomach into
backflips.

"And so I would have invited one of the other gentlemen,
had Lord Tristram declined." Mama stood at a refectory
table at one end of the room, arranging flowers in a crystal bowl, chrysanthemums in shades of orange, gold and
yellow sent up fresh from the city. The arrangement would
grace the center of the table. Other smaller bowls already
stood on tables throughout the public rooms.

If only she could wear her gold gown from Paris. Catherine lamented being unable to show at her best if she had to help play hostess to Tristram. It would show well with the color theme Mama had chosen for the dinner party decor. Instead, she would behave herself and wear a velvet gown of such deep purple it looked black away from direct lighting. Perhaps a little gold jewelry would set it off nicely. Just a little and, with Tristram coming, only pieces she owned before or since her time in England.

"I don't know why you two are objecting to his lordship," Mama said.

"He's not truly a lord, you know." Catherine had spent months learning how the English peerage worked. "He's still a commoner."

"Unless his sister-in-law produces a girl." Estelle made the comment without looking up from her scribbling on the musical score.

Catherine startled. "What do you mean? He has an older brother."

Estelle glanced up. "You didn't know? His brother died seven months ago."

Long enough for him to be out of mourning for a sibling.

"I didn't know." Catherine shook her head. "I left England a year ago August and had as little as possible to do with anyone from the English aristocracy."

"You need to rid your heart of this bitterness, Catherine." Mama's dark eyes clouded with sadness. "I'm certain they aren't all like your husband."

Catherine grimaced. "Lord Tristram's older brother was."

"He'd been drinking heavily and fell from his horse," Estelle confirmed. "Mr. Wolfe told me so I'd know that he's only third in line to the title if Lady, um—what's her name?"

"Her husband's courtesy title was Harriford."

In one of the two times she'd been able to go to London, Catherine had seen the lady in a dressmaker's shop. She was a pretty, petite blonde with a sweet-faced daughter in tow. She had been apologizing to a shopgirl for how badly the young woman's employer had been treating her for some imagined slight to her ladyship, a genuine kindness from a lady who deserved better than the current heir to the Marquess of Cothbridge.

"I hope for her sake," Catherine mused aloud, "she has a girl. That will free her to marry someone more of her choosing. But if she has a boy, she'll be stranded at Cothbridge and under the marquess's thumb."

"If she has a girl," Estelle pointed out, "Lord Tristram will inherit the title."

"Which is likely why he's here in America." Mama took a half dozen steps back from her flower arrangement. "He's looking to find an American heiress."

"He doesn't need an heiress if he inherits," Catherine said. "The Wolfes are quite wealthy. Why would he need a separate income?"

"Apparently," Estelle explained, "his father is so angry with him for resigning his army commission he has cut him off unless he does something important."

Catherine's finger slipped, and she jabbed her embroidery needle into her finger.

"How romantic." Mama returned to her flowers and began to tuck greenery around the edges of the bowl. "What sort of important thing must he do?"

Estelle furrowed her brow, wrote something on her score, then glanced up long enough to say, "I don't know. Mr. Wolfe wouldn't tell me, if he even knows."

Oh, he knew, as did Catherine. He needed to prove she was a thief and procure the rest of the jewelry she did not have. Probably even recover the money made on selling the other pieces in Europe, which she, of course, didn't have because she had never obtained it.

And now Mama had invited him to dinner and he had accepted. Of course he had accepted.

An absurd image flashed through her mind—Lord Tristram Wolfe slipping up the servants' steps to her bedchamber, rifling through her jewel box.

"Could you not invite Mr. Wolfe and Mr. Baston-Ward to the party, as well?" Estelle was asking.

"I'd have had to find two more single ladies in that event." Mama swept across the room to the bell. "Mr. Harold Padget already accepted my invitation, so when Mr. Rutlidge couldn't come, I had to scramble for another bachelor to make the table even."

Estelle heaved a sigh strong enough to have fanned the flames on the hearth had she sat closer to the fire. "I suppose Mr. Loring is for me?"

Which meant Tristram would escort Catherine into dinner instead of her brother.

"He is quite unexceptionable as a suitor, Estelle." Mama directed her attention to the footman who had responded to her ring, directing him to carry the crystal bowl of flowers out of the room. Mama followed, no doubt to supervise its placement on the table.

Estelle covered her eyes with her hand. "Mr. Loring is nearly twice my age and doesn't know an A from an F. I've heard him try to sing in church."

Catherine examined her finger for blood and resumed her embroidery. "Well, Lord Tristram doesn't like me."

"Ha." Estelle flashed Catherine a grin. "That's not how it looked in the music room the other day. He couldn't take his eyes off of you."

"Probably afraid I'd steal his tiepin," Catherine muttered.

"What did you say?"

"Never mind." Catherine set her needlework into its basket and lifted the handle. "I'm going for a walk. Do you want to join me?"

Estelle glanced out the window at the pale blue sky free of clouds. "I don't wish to risk chapping my hands. I'm going to go practice before Mama returns and finds something for me to do for this party. It is going to be so very dull if I have to entertain Mr. Loring."

"Unless you attach yourself to the ladies planning the charity tea."

"It's a good notion." Estelle slipped through the narrow door leading to the music room.

Catherine climbed to her room to fetch a hat and coat for a brisk walk along the lakeshore. She had grown fond of walking during her years in England. It got her away from the never-ending hammering and sawing as her money repaired the manor. Only the rainiest days kept her inside, and she had kept up the practice once back in New York.

She set off down the path leading to the lake. Though the sun blazed across the sky, ice still rimmed the lake, shiny on top where the surface had thawed. In no time, they would be able to ice-skate or toboggan. She gave a little hop of excitement at the prospect. Ice and snow were as foreign to Romney Marsh as she had been. Soon, perhaps, if she could make her peace with Georgette, Tuxedo Park would be home again. But Georgette hadn't responded to any of her notes. Between that and Lord Tristram being determined to ruin her, she was beginning to doubt that anywhere could be home.

"Lord Jesus, feeling settled somewhere isn't too much to ask, is it?" she said aloud.

Catherine didn't pray a great deal. Perhaps she should, yet now, when her heart ached over the unfair accusation and the not-so-subtle messages that Georgette still wished for nothing to do with her, seemed wrong. If she wasn't going to keep in contact with the Lord in good times, then she shouldn't ask Him for help during the bad.

Guilt and cold air constricted her breathing. Even Estelle, who would disobey their parents with the first opportunity to become a professional musician, could write a song called "Praise." Perhaps the best alternative was a combination of prayer and request? "Hallowed be Thy name" and "Give us this day our daily bread" in equal measure?

Contemplations on prayer needed to wait. If she didn't head home, only a miracle would get her ready for the party on time.

And tonight, preparing for the party meant more than donning an evening gown and choosing appropriate jewelry that would not bring the wrong kind of attention.

It meant working out exactly how to manage Lord Tristram Wolfe.

Tristram's mouth went dry at the sight of Lady Bisterne. In a purple gown that emphasized her long neck surrounded by a necklace of flat gold and enamel plaques, she looked like a queen.

If Edwin Bisterne had married her only for her fortune, then he had been a bigger fool than Tristram believed. If he'd married her only for her money, then perhaps he owed her those jewels after all.

Poised in the doorway to the VanDorns' drawing room for half a minute longer than he should have been, Tristram watched Catherine ministering to the oldest guests. She tucked a pillow behind the back of an aged matron he already knew from experience was more than a little crotchety, then she glided across the floor to move a fire screen to better reflect heat for an old man with twinkling eyes. A middle-aged gentleman caught her hand as she passed. Instead of giving him the set-down he deserved, she offered him a brilliant smile, said something that not only made him release her fingers, but laugh while he let her go.

Tristram's conscience bit deep. Believing her guilty of revenge theft, especially once he realized how much she disliked her husband, was easy when he wasn't with her. But this gracious and elegant lady could surely not so much as contemplate stealing her wedding ring on purpose, let alone an entire vault full of jewelry.

And yet...

Deciding he had been the fool this night for accepting the invitation, he entered the drawing room. Mr. VanDorn came toward him, one hand extended in greeting, the other holding a cup from which steam wafted.

"Hot cider after what was surely a cold ride over." Mr. VanDorn gave Tristram the glass.

"I walked." Tristram took the cup and wrapped his hands around it. "I enjoy walking, weather permitting."

"You sound like my daughter." His gaze flicked across the room toward Catherine. "Which reminds me, she is your dinner partner."

Of course she was. Social precedent dictated the two of them would be seated either across from or next to one another. No doubt his hostess would be on the other side.

"Allow me to make a few introductions for you." Van-Dorn set his hand on Tristram's shoulder. Then he proceeded to introduce people with names Tristram recognized because they occasionally made news in the English papers.

"Dinner's about to be announced," Mr. VanDorn said, "so I'll leave you with my eldest daughter."

The circuit of the room had ended in front of Catherine and more windows offering a spectacular view of the lake beneath a full moon. She stood close enough to the window that her breath fogged the glass, blurring her reflection. His was perfectly clear beside hers.

"Good evening, Lord Tristram." She raised one hand,

on which sparkled an amethyst ring the size of a quail egg. The scent of spring swirled around her, violets and lily of the valley.

Tristram found he could think of nothing to say. He watched her reach toward the glass, half expecting her to write in the steam. Instead, she started to use the lace frill at the bottom of her sleeve.

"Allow me." He reached past her and wiped the glass with his handkerchief.

She faced him. "Why did you come?"

"I can't ferret out your secrets if I don't ever see you."

"All you will learn is that I have no secrets." Indeed, her brown eyes were wide and as guileless as a child's.

Too guileless.

He gave her his own limpid gaze. "We shall see. I—"

The dinner bell rang, and couples began to form.

Tristram offered her his arm. For a moment, she remained motionless, as though she were about to refuse his offer. Then, as the last of the other couples left the drawing room, she laid her fingertips on his forearm. Just her fingertips.

She may as well have pressed hard upon the nerves in his forearm. He needed all his self-control not to jerk away a reaction that must be wholly wrong. He was pursuing her, not courting her.

He reached the dining room on feet that felt as though he wore large Wellington boots rather than light evening shoes. To his relief, she released his arm the instant they reached their places.

A footman drew out her chair. She settled into it with fluid grace. As soon as Mr. VanDorn asked the blessing over the meal, Catherine turned to the gentleman on her right, leaving Tristram to his hostess through the soup course. Mrs. VanDorn was practiced at polite dialogue, asking him questions about his family, then his work.

"Though I suppose you don't work, do you? So different between England and America. Here, even the men in our best families work."

"Besides some charity work, I've been helping my father manage his land holdings since my brother's passing. That, ma'am, is a great deal of work."

"Oh, and how much land is that?" Her tone suggested it was no bigger than a farm.

"Twenty thousand acres."

She choked on her sip of soup.

"It's a respectable size." For no good reason, he wanted her to know his branch of the family had enough money that he didn't need an heiress. "Nothing like what you have out in the west."

"But more civilized."

Their rapport after that was quite good. Mrs. VanDorn, Tristram couldn't help but notice, was a fine image of what Catherine would look like in twenty years—poised and still beautiful with those fine bones.

Catherine would remain beautiful if she didn't let her anger over her husband etch lines of bitterness into her face. Her mother was a happy woman who glowed whenever she mentioned the name of one of her children.

Pure motherly pride…that he could shatter.

He felt like a hypocrite eating at her table.

When the salad course arrived and Mrs. VanDorn turned to the man on her left, Tristram switched his attention to Catherine. She stabbed a strip of lettuce and moved it from one side to the other, set her fork down, sipped water, then resumed the lettuce relocation process. Not once did she so much as take a bite or glance at him.

"Isn't not speaking to me unforgivably rude?" Her actions finally pressed him to ask.

"Isn't coming to the home of people whose daughter you've accused of theft unforgivably rude?"

He winced. "I could end up proving your innocence, too, you know."

"You could choose to believe me." She set down her fork and gave up the pretense of eating.

"Please, let us converse like civilized beings." Beneath the edge of the tablecloth, he pressed his right hand over her left.

Her hand twitched, but she did not draw it away. "I'm rather out of practice with social repartee."

"Tell me about your favorite places on the continent."

"The Alps?" She sounded uncertain, her words tentative. "We have magnificent mountains in this country, though I have never seen them, but the Alps were... Well, who needs a cathedral for worship when one has places like that?"

"You prefer the mountains to Florence or Rome?"

"I do. Paintings are all well and good, but nature..." Her hesitation vanished the more she talked, and by the end of the meal, when Mrs. VanDorn rose to lead the ladies from the room, he had discovered many interests he and Catherine shared—land, quiet and things of beauty, such as soaring mountains and well-written books. She was pretty, intelligent and in possession of a gift for witty observation. Under other circumstances, he would love to spend more time in her company.

In truth, he would love to spend more time in her company regardless of the circumstances. Indeed, with her clear, cultured voice still caressing his ears, he perhaps should consider proving her innocence rather than her guilt. Surely a lady who appreciated God's creation over man's wouldn't hold much stock in jewels. Yet the evidence against her was rather strong.

He wanted to pursue her and talk to her with less antagonism than they had shared when the subject of the jewels was their subject of dialogue. For now, he was stranded in the dining room with a dozen men he barely knew. The

VanDorns were an abstemious family, so coffee and tea were the only beverages. Tristram accepted a cup of excellent tea, and leaned back in his chair. Knowing too little of American politics to join in the discussion of President McKinley's reelection the day before, Tristram listened with partial concentration, mainly concerned with how he should proceed with his investigation into Catherine and the jewels.

By the time Mr. VanDorn suggested they join the ladies, Tristram had his answer.

Chapter 7

The ideal partner is one who never criticizes or even seems to be aware of your mistakes, but on the contrary recognizes a good maneuver on your part, and gives you credit for it whether you win the hand or lose…

Emily Price Post

Tristram found Catherine dispensing coffee and tea from a low table at one end of the drawing room. Estelle carried the cups to ladies settled in groups around the chamber. When Tristram approached Catherine, she slid a cup of tea toward him without looking higher than the middle button on his waistcoat.

"I don't care for more tea." He glanced around for a chair but the nearest seat was the other cushion of the settee on which she perched. "May I?"

"You may, though I see two empty chairs by the window."

"Will you join me there so I may talk with you some more?"

"I must pour the tea. So sit if you must."

"Not particularly gracious, but I accept." For her sake, he sat as far from her as the small sofa allowed.

"I didn't think you would do that."

"Why not?"

"You wouldn't want anyone to think you're paying special attention to me." She spoke in an undertone.

"No one will think it odd."

"Perhaps not." She lifted the coffeepot and started to pour.

"No more," Estelle said, approaching the table. "Some people are leaving. I shall entertain the rest of the guests." She sailed off for the music room, her fingers moving at her sides as though she already played an instrument.

"Excellent. No interruptions." Tristram half turned on the settee so he could see Catherine better.

With a number of the remaining guests casting speculative glances in their direction, she could remain as she was, stiff-backed, hands folded in her lap, giving him her profile; stand and leave; or angle herself so they could talk more directly. The first two choices would be unforgivably rude from a social perspective, and subject for gossip. The third option, however, could lead to gossip that he was courting her or, at the least, entering into a flirtation.

She took so long to move, he feared she would risk rudeness. Then, just as the strains of a violin began to drift from the music room, and he was considering bidding good-night to save her embarrassment, she picked up the cup he had rejected and turned just enough to hand it to him.

"Drink your fill." She set the cup and saucer into his hands. "If I remember correctly, the Selkirks' cook makes terrible tea—by English standards."

"Nothing has changed." Although more tea would keep him up for hours, he sipped the tea, inhaling the fragrance of bergamot blended with Catherine's spring flower scent, the latter as likely to keep him awake as the former. "I considered purchasing a spirit lamp and tea in the city so I could make my own in my room."

"I'd like to see the old lady's face if you had." She laughed.

He warmed to his toes. "A gross breach of etiquette?"

"You might get away with it as simple English eccentricity."

"Then I should have done so." He set the cup and saucer back on the table, wanting nothing but clear air between them. "Or may I come here whenever I need a cup of real tea?"

Her folded hands clenched. "You don't wish to do that."

"Ah, but I do."

"Why?" She slid so close to the edge of her cushion he feared she would tumble to the flowered carpet.

He rested one hand on the back of the settee, too far from her shoulders for the gesture to be inappropriately intimate, but hinting to the others in the room that he intended this conversation to remain private in plain sight. "I made an important decision after you left the dining room."

She merely arched one brow in a question.

"If it weren't for the jewels, we'd get on fairly well—"

"But there are the jewels of which I am innocent of stealing."

"And I am obligated to prove otherwise. So I believe the only solution for either of us is that I become one of your greatest admirers."

"You intend to what?" The others in the room might have been able to hear her exclamation if the violin recital hadn't exploded into a lively gypsy melody.

He grinned. "I intend to become one of your greatest—"

"I heard you the first time." Voice lowered, she held a hand in the air to stop him from repeating himself. "I meant what do you think you're playing at with such a suggestion?"

"No game."

"Ha. Your very presence here is some kind of game. Did the Baston-Ward family put you up to it? Did they… Did they…" She struggled, then her eyes narrowed. "Did they send someone to sell the jewels in my wake to make me look guilty in order to extort funds from me?"

"A thought I hadn't considered." The violin dropped into something slow and dreamlike, and he lowered his voice to a mere murmur. "With good reason. The jewels were missing when the new earl first opened the safe."

"And do you only have their word for it?"

"I have my father's word for it. And since my father has nothing to gain here, and a great deal to lose financially, I am taking his word over yours."

"Then you are hoping for the opportunity to sneak into my room and search my jewel case?"

"I expect you're too good a player to keep the jewels near your person." He rose and bowed. "I shall call on you as soon as my host's plans permit." He started to turn away.

"I won't be at home." He barely heard her above the lively Scottish tune Estelle had begun to play. "Unless you're willing to perform a service for me in return."

If he could gain her cooperation without a struggle, he would do anything he could, even if it meant he ran the risk of incurring his earthly father's wrath. It was a small price to pay for extending grace to her as would his heavenly Father.

"And what is that?"

She lifted her gaze to his, and the cocoa-dark eyes looked as soft as her gown. "Arrange a meeting for me with Georgette Selkirk."

"You want me to arrange a meeting with Miss—" He paused and glanced toward the rest of the company. The violin had ceased and the remaining guests had all risen in preparation to leave. Anyone could overhear their conversation now.

"Do you have any histories I may borrow?" He posed the question so abruptly she looked as startled as he felt, but he plunged on. "I'm afraid my host's books run to novels, and I wish to know more about, hmm…" He faltered.

She rose, a twinkle setting gold lights dancing in her eyes. "History, perhaps? American history, that is. We have a book by Moses King on the history of New York. Will that do?"

"Quite well, thank you." He offered her his arm.

After the merest hint of a hesitation, she took it. As he led her from the drawing room, he fought an urge to cover her fingers with his, press them more firmly onto his forearm. He shoved his free hand into his coat pocket to stop himself from being so foolish.

As though she knew of his considered impulse, she released his arm the instant they stepped into the library, and swept across the room to remove a leather-bound volume from a shelf. "This should give you some information." She held out the book.

He took it and held it between both hands. "Why do you wish to speak to Miss Selkirk?"

Catherine ran her fingers across her necklace, lifting it from her throat, her eyes fixed past his shoulder. "I need to ask her forgiveness. I need to do what I can to make amends for the past, for what I…I did to her."

And after how the Selkirks had treated her. His heart turned to warm clay Catherine could have molded in her elegant hands. Dangerous to feel so strongly in her favor. He was working against her.

"Not admirable," Catherine said. "Necessary. If I'm ever going to do anything useful with my life, I can't have the past hanging over me like this."

"Useful?" He had met few society ladies on either side of the Atlantic who spoke of making their lives useful. "How?"

"I don't yet know." She wrinkled her nose and laughed

with an edge. "Let me clear my conscience and my name first."

"And I can help with both." He took a step toward her. "I fully understand wishing to be useful. If I—"

She turned abruptly enough for her skirt to swing out and brush against his ankles. "I hope that book suits." She stepped into the foyer, where the butler assisted a lady into her coat. "Good night, Lord Tristram. I am certain we will meet again."

"Indeed." He bowed. "I will do my best to fulfill your request." He departed with a sense of dissatisfaction over their conversation. He wanted to—needed to—tell her so much more than he had, explain about his father and his mission so she would understand why he pursued her.

Another day. He would get Georgette to call on Catherine to give himself another day.

It was a foolish promise for him to make. Although he saw Georgette daily, he rarely spoke to her alone for more than a minute or two. He couldn't bring up such a personal issue in the constant presence of others, though was tempted to broach the topic in the middle of a dinner party waltz with Georgette's undivided attention so close at hand. Except in the middle of that waltz with Georgette, he caught sight of Catherine across the room and instead found himself wishing he was spinning her around the drawing room turned dance floor.

He saw her in snatches, brief dialogues in the great hall clubhouse, or on the veranda, where she drank tea with some local ladies in the warm autumn sun, or at the home of someone bold enough to invite Selkirks and VanDorns together. He never mentioned the jewels. She never mentioned Georgette, and he walked away feeling as though the exchanges held more value than hours spent in others' company. Each exchange showed him a lady who loved her family, found beauty even in a rainy day and still wanted to do something useful with her life. When the Selkirks decided to return to the city, reluctantly, Florian, Ambrose and Tristram went along, as they had little choice with their host and the female family members going.

"I'll do some hunting through the jewelry and pawnshops." Ambrose gave Tristram a pointed glare. "Since you seem to have given up the hunt. Perhaps your father will give *me* the reward if I prove the woman took the jewels and get the rest back."

"Not to mention the money she got for the ones she sold." Florian frowned. "Though I admit I'm finding it harder and harder to believe she's guilty. She so quiet and kind."

"And she's Estelle's sister." Ambrose cuffed him on the shoulder.

"In spite of the fact that we've made this horrible accusation against her," Florian said, "Lady Bisterne still treats us with all that's gracious."

"Don't trust her." Ambrose snapped out the words. "Remember how she schemed to get Bisterne away from Miss Selkirk."

Tristram's upper lip curled. "I doubt he needed much persuasion once he learned the size of her dowry outshone Miss Selkirk's."

"And she's nearly as pretty as her sister." Florian cast an oblique glance at Tristram. "Don't you think, Tris?"

"Prettier." The word slipped out before he could stop himself.

Both his companions stared at him.

"No wonder you've stopped trying to get the jewelry back," Ambrose murmured. "You're besotted with her."

"You'd better tell the beauteous Georgette," Florian added. "She has her cap firmly set in your direction."

"Don't be absurd." Tristram shrugged off their remarks

with more nonchalance than he felt. "We scarcely know one another."

But in his heart, Tristram did not quite believe this to be true. He was beginning to feel he knew Catherine well enough that it was unnerving, given what he'd come to America to do.

On their third day in the city, Ambrose and Florian had gone to witness some low form of entertainment in the area known as the Bowery. Pierce had accompanied his mother and grandmother to visit their dressmaker, and Georgette had stayed behind.

"It's too fine a day to stay indoors getting poked and prodded and stuck full of pins." Georgette gave Tristram a pointed glance. "I can persuade you to take me to the park for a brisk walk, can I not?"

"You can." Tristram, too, welcomed a long, fast walk through the park.

While Georgette fetched her coat and hat, and for the first hundred yards out the Selkirks' front door, Tristram thought about Catherine's request. Was this his opportunity to ask Georgette if she'd meet with Catherine? How would she respond? Or was it not his place to say anything at all about Lady Bisterne?

"I never realized you are so shy," Georgette said, breaking the silence. "You never seem at a loss when Pierce is with us."

Tristram's ears heated despite the biting wind blowing from the west. "I haven't spent a great deal of time with young, pretty females between school, university and then the army."

"You place me in that category?" She tilted her head to peek up at him from beneath the wide brim of her hat.

"I should think your mirror tells you the truth of that every day."

Georgette heaved a sigh audible above the cries of children playing a game of tag beside the path.

"I've seen how the men wish to dance with you," he added.

"Men I've known all my life." She wrinkled her nose as the fallen, dried leaves carpeting the path crunched under their feet. "I'm considering going to Europe to find some variety. Of course, having variety come to us has helped my ennui a great deal." She pressed her fingers into his arm.

"We appreciate the hospitality of your family." Tristram hesitated, then plunged in. "Everyone in Tuxedo Park has been cordial and welcoming. I've quite enjoyed many of the entertainments, including at the VanDorns'."

"Of course you have." The corners of her mouth drooped. "Mrs. VanDorn sets a fine table and none of them is anything but intelligent and kind."

"Including Lady Bisterne?" The instant he spoke the title Georgette had lost, he regretted it, but he could scarcely call her Catherine aloud.

Georgette paused on the path and gazed out across a pond. "Catherine has well paid for her actions of five years ago."

"She would like to speak with you. She asked me if I would affect a meeting."

She spun to face him. "Why?"

"I believe she feels badly—"

Her shoulders tensed. "No, no, why did she ask you to play envoy?"

"Because I was available."

The tension eased, and she smiled. "In that event, I will call on her as soon as I may after we return."

"I will be happy to escort—"

"No." One sharp word, then she grasped his arm and started walking. "My family wouldn't approve."

After they returned from their walk, the remark rattled

around inside his head, and it continued to do so for the next several days, during which he suddenly found himself alone in Georgette's company more than strictly proper. The truth he suspected became clear.

The Selkirks were working hard to fix his attentions on Georgette.

He didn't need to question why. The Selkirks wanted his title in the family. It presented quite a conundrum. If he sought out Catherine, he could ruin her chance at reconciling with Georgette. Yet if he did not spend time with Catherine, he might never learn the truth behind the missing jewels, in which case his own reconciliation with his father, not to mention the reclaiming of wealth on which scores of people relied, would be lost.

And then there was the small matter of how he felt when days went by during which he did not get to spend time with Lady Bisterne…

A conundrum indeed.

What nonsense Catherine had spoken when she'd declared she would be happy to be at home the next time Lord Tristram Wolfe called. Nothing about the man made her happy. On the contrary, being near him left her restless and dissatisfied with…what? The brevity of their surprisingly delightful dialogues? That he didn't call again for another week and a half made her angry, when in fact, the lack of lengthy contact should have made her happy.

Until the past few days, Florian and Ambrose had visited far more often than was proper. Since they spent all that time in the music room with Estelle, the sessions seemed harmless enough. What was not harmless was how often Estelle danced with Florian at entertainments that offered that activity. But her sister laughed off Catherine's concerns and lamented that the three of them had nowhere to perform the pieces they had been working on.

"Music should not be hidden behind closed doors," Estelle declared.

"But, child," Mama protested, "you are a debutante. You can't perform in public."

"I did at the ball and—"

"Wait." Catherine lifted her hand from the list of Tuxedo Park residents she was going over for invitations to a charity tea the week after Thanksgiving Day. "I don't see why they can't entertain the guests at the tea. We can spend more money on gifts for the children if we don't have to pay professional entertainers to provide the music."

"I don't know." Mama frowned.

Estelle leaped to her feet and hugged Catherine. "Thank you, thank you! Are you inviting Lord Tristram? It would seem appropriate if his friends are the entertainment."

"I'll be sending an invitation to the Selkirks, of course. All the residents will be receiving one." She bent her head over her list. "Not that I expect anyone from that house to attend."

Estelle poked Catherine's arm. "I should think Lord Tristram would come. The two of you look rather friendly when you meet."

"And he and Georgette looked rather cozy at Mrs. Vanderleyden's soiree." Catherine chose to blame the unpleasant squeezing of her middle that she felt at this memory on her regret that she and Georgette hadn't so much as made eye contact at the event.

Five years ago, they would have dragged one another off to discuss their plans for the evening before facing the crowd—the young men—together. Now Catherine found herself thanking the Lord that Georgette's grandmother hadn't come along to create a scene when the poet Mrs. Vanderleyden had invited to entertain her guests had failed to arrive on the train. She'd substituted dancing with music provided by some of her servants.

"He's obligated to play the gallant to the sister of his host," Mama pointed out. "But if he comes to the tea, you may reacquaint yourselves."

"Not that Catherine wants another Englishman for a husband."

Catherine scowled at her sister. "Not that Catherine wants another husband. I am making myself quite content helping Mama plan this tea. And Mrs. Rutledge has asked me to help her plan her annual Christmas charity ball in the city. She hasn't been well and thinks, because I lived in Europe for five years, I should know about all that is fashionable and refined." She laughed.

Mama's face lit. "Catherine, that is wonderful. What an honor."

"Even if she *is* quite mistaken about your life overseas." Estelle executed a pirouette and ended up at the door to the music room. "I must see what music will be suitable for the tea. Something proper for the month of Christmas, yes? May I send a note around to Fl— Mr. Baston-Ward and Mr. Wolfe?"

"I shall do so on your behalf." Mama rose from the sofa where she worked at a bit of embroidery. "Catherine, may I use the desk?"

"I'll go into the library." Catherine gathered up her lists and moved next door to the library.

Scents of leather from the hundreds of books lining the shelves and the heavy, masculine furniture contrasted with the sweet orange aroma from the oil rubbed into the desk. It gleamed beneath sunlight streaming through the windows that provided warmth, despite the frigid outside temperature.

The sun wouldn't last for long. Clouds piling up in the north predicted sleet or snow before evening. Catherine hoped it would arrive late enough that Papa and Paul didn't get stranded in the city, but early enough that night's entertainment would be canceled.

It was a dance strictly for young people and she had been designated to be Estelle's chaperone. She wanted something to do with her life, but acting as if she was forty-four rather than twenty-four was unacceptable. Whether she wanted to or not, Estelle would marry within a year or two, and then what would Catherine do? Her parents were too young to need her to stay with them. And she was too used to running her own household to be happy living with Mama's management.

For now, she was happy to plan the two charity events. The invitations to the tea needed to go out within the next day or two and decisions needed to be made. Should she send Lord Tristram a separate invitation, so he could attend even if the Selkirks refused? Other than brief conversations around Tuxedo Park, Tristram hadn't tried to contact her, from which she concluded he had been unable to persuade Georgette to call on Catherine. Her heart heavy, she bent to the task of addressing envelopes for the tea.

Mrs. Paul VanDorn II and Lady Catherine Bisterne invite you…

A discreet notation in the bottom corner of the return card indicated the minimum donation the attendee was to include in the *Répondez, s'il vous plaît* envelope.

As she wrote, the muted strains of Estelle's banjo penetrated the wall of books, but it was not the smooth, liquid way in which she played. This musician was inexpert with the instrument. Estelle must be teaching someone—Florian and Ambrose must have called.

She'd gotten so used to the men coming over to play in the afternoons, she paid them little attention. She didn't approve, but she had, after all, recommended Mama not interfere and let the novelty of the Englishmen run its course.

The last invitation addressed and sealed, she rose and stretched. The sun had vanished and a chill penetrated the chamber.

So did silence.

Catherine tilted her head and listened. Not a sound save for the wind sighing through the trees.

Uneasiness took hold as she left the room and slipped into the drawing room next door. Mama and her needlework had gone. The music room door stood open.

Catherine crossed to stand in the doorway.

Florian perched on the piano stool. Estelle stood before him. One of his hands held the banjo. The other curled around Estelle's fingers as they gazed into one another's eyes.

A hundred words of remonstrance rose in Catherine's throat but none emerged. The bitter ache of longing for someone to look at her with adoration, as Florian gazed at Estelle, blocked their way. Edwin had never once looked at Catherine like that.

As quietly as she could, Catherine took a step back and turned away. Her skirt rustled, but not loudly enough to interrupt the two young people.

She found Mama in the housekeeper's room discussing arrangements for the tea. Perhaps Catherine's face showed her agitation, for the housekeeper rose with some excuse about ensuring they didn't need any provisions from the village before the storm hit in full, and left Catherine and Mama alone.

"I'm afraid Florian and Estelle are developing an affection for one another," Catherine blurted.

"I know." Mama toyed with her fountain pen. "It's not the sort of match we would like for her, but if it dispels this notion of becoming a musician, so be it. He seems to be a nice young man."

"He is. Or at least I never heard of him engaging in riotous living, and he's been coming to church, but he has no prospects. He's too much of a gentleman to work."

"So, my dear, was your husband, yet you saw fit to elope with him." The rebuke stung.

Catherine turned away. "I thought a title and land were enough. Now I know so much more is necessary for a husband. I doubt I'll ever find another one."

"You will if it's what the Lord has for you." Mama's voice was gentle. "Lord Tristram—"

"Has no interest in me." Catherine cut off her mother before she could suggest he was a potential mate. "And he's not only English, he's potentially heir to a title. Once was quite enough for me with regard to all that. Now I shall go chaperone those two before hand-holding leads to something inappropriate."

She reached the corridor just as Florian prepared to leave. Estelle, rather than a footman, was handing him his hat and gloves.

He started to clasp Estelle's fingers, then saw Catherine and drew back. "Lady Bisterne, how do you do?"

"Fine, thank you. Where is Ambrose?"

"He's in the city with the Selkirks." Florian grinned. "Seems he met some minor heiress there he's thinking of courting. But we got bored squiring the ladies around to all their shopping, so Tris and Pierce and I came back this morning."

No wonder she hadn't seen any of them even from a distance for several days. Perhaps now Tristram would call. She wished she could think of a message for Florian to give Tristram, but she did not want to raise any curiosity, so she said goodbye and returned to the library.

The floor-to-ceiling windows framed the first flakes

of snow beginning to fall. Catherine curled up on a chair before the fire and read as the storm turned into the first significant snowfall of the season, a white curtain so thick it blocked the view of the lake. Papa called to say he and Paul would stay at their club in the city. As night fell, the wind rose, howling around corners and rattling the windows. Estelle played the piano with thunderous chords to match the blizzard, and Mama went to bed early complaining of drafts.

Catherine returned to the library alone, where she sat and paced at intervals, trying to shake off the sense that the snow piled atop her like rocks. "Lord," she said aloud for the sound of a human voice, "being here like this is unacceptable."

She should talk to Estelle about her closeness with Florian. That, too, was unacceptable. They were alone—alone together, a couple.

Catherine slammed her palms to the sides of her head. Surely she wasn't jealous of Estelle and Florian finding one another. No, no, she was concerned about Estelle marrying a fortune hunter, one who didn't even have a home of his own. She didn't want her younger sister to suffer as she had. And yet Florian looked at Estelle with a tenderness Catherine never received from her husband.

And that hurt as well, hurt as had the sight of Tristram dancing with Georgette.

Wait. She hadn't cared about that. He thought Catherine a jewel thief. She should despise him, be happy he attended to escorting Georgette around the Park—and the city. Georgette hadn't been alone for days. She was going to walk off with the English title this time. Tristram was no Bisterne. He would be kind to Georgette, as he had been kind to Catherine even while accusing her—

She thrust speculations about Georgette and Tristram, Florian and Estelle aside—or tried to.

Once Estelle went to bed, the two couples began to whirl through Catherine's mind again. The emptiness grew as bad as being at Bisterne—a house full of servants and her heart aching with loneliness. Unable to face her bedroom, she remained in the library reading to block all else from her mind, until the wind died down and that peculiar hush of snowfall blanketed the world.

And she could bear the stillness no longer.

As quietly as she could, she raced up the steps to the third floor and the cedar-lined room in which they kept winter garments. From a corner, she unearthed her old fur-lined boots and muff. After slipping downstairs again, she donned the boots and bundled up in a hat, scarf and warm coat. Then she let herself outside through one of the library's French doors.

All her life she'd adored being the first person to leave footprints in pristine snow. She might even toss off her veneer of staid widow and create a snow angel for the household to wonder over in the morning. Laughing softly, she stepped off the veranda toward the edge of the lake. It turned out hers were not the first footprints to mar the snow's perfection.

By the light of a clearing sky full of stars, she caught sight of deep impressions in the white carpet, impressions twice the size of hers.

Her heart sank at the idea that a man had intruded upon her private moments of freedom. Getting inside the fence around Tuxedo Park wasn't easy, but it could be done. Most visitors were perfectly all right, though a woman alone at night must be careful.

She started to turn back to the house when she noticed that the footprints stopped near the shoreline. And where they ceased lay the body of a man, crumpled against the trunk of a spruce.

Chapter 8

The well-bred maid instinctively makes little of a guest's accident, and is as considerate as the hostess herself. Employees instinctively adopt the attitude of their employer.

Emily Price Post

Though the sky was clear, the stars weren't bright enough for Catherine to distinguish the identity of the fallen man. Whether village worker, park resident or someone's servant, he needed help and quickly. When she reached him, she stooped to check his pulse. Finding one, she pulled off her coat and tossed it over him, then she raced for the house as quickly as six inches of snow allowed.

Every room was dark save for the library and her own chamber. She didn't feel comfortable going into the servants' quarters, but Sapphire would be in Catherine's chamber waiting to help her undress. She headed there, taking the steps two at a time, and flung open the door.

"Sapphire, we need two footmen and perhaps the housekeeper. Hot water. Perhaps bandages."

"Indeed, m'lady?" Sapphire set aside her knitting and rose from her seat by the fire. "Who is injured?"

"I don't know. I found him in the snow just now."

"The snow, m'lady?" Sapphire arched her finely plucked

brows. "We will need a room made up for him, then. Servants' quarters or guest room?"

Catherine pressed a hand to her racing heart. "I won't know until we get him into the light."

"Then we had best do so quickly. Who knows how long he's been in the cold." With an easy stride that seemed slow but covered a great deal of ground with each step, Sapphire headed for the back steps.

Catherine grabbed a cashmere shawl from a drawer and raced back into the snow. The man still lay there in a heap like a discarded rag doll. His pulse beat in his neck, but it was slow and his skin felt barely warmer than the snow around her. With no idea what to do until the footmen arrived, she rubbed his cheeks with the fur muff warmed from her hands. Once, she heard him groan. But mostly she heard her own ragged breathing sending white puffs of steam into the air. She sent a prayer heavenward for his well-being, whoever he was.

She didn't realize how loudly she prayed until Sapphire arrived without Catherine hearing her, and rested a hand on her shoulder. "We're here, m'lady. Let us take him in through the library so we can assess his condition and station."

"No, he needs to get warm swiftly. Take him straight to a guest room."

The footman looked at her askance, but Sapphire merely nodded, and when they reached the house, she led the way up to the second floor, where a maid was building a fire on the hearth.

"Sapphire," Catherine said, "do you think of everything?"

"It's my duty, m'lady. I guessed you would want the man here regardless of his station. I have also sent for Dr. Rushmore."

"Of course you did." Catherine stepped out of the doorway so the footmen could lay their burden on the bed.

Light from a bedside lamp fell on the injured man's face. Catherine grasped the back of a nearby chair for support, a gasp escaping her lips.

"Lord Tristram!"

For a moment, the gold-tipped lashes swept upward, revealing eyes that lacked light, his face ashen. "You look like an angel." He smiled, then his eyes closed again.

Suddenly too warm in her white cashmere shawl, Catherine backed out the doorway. "We will leave you men to remove his wet garments and make him comfortable." She turned on her heel and fled downstairs to wait for the doctor, to call Florian and Pierce, to forget he had called her an angel.

It meant nothing. He knew her as anything but something pure and good. He wanted to prove her even worse than a mere selfish creature. Now that he was in the house, was this his opportunity? If someone was wily enough to plant the jewels in shops along her route through Europe, she wouldn't put it past the real thief to sneak into her house and place one of the stolen pieces of jewelry in her dressing table.

Given half a chance, she would have Lord Tristram moved back to the Selkirks immediately.

But he couldn't be moved, according to Dr. Rushmore when Catherine, Mama and Estelle sat in the conservatory with him an hour later. "Slight concussion. Looks like he slipped in the snow and hit his head on that tree."

"What was he doing on our lawn?" Mama asked.

He shook his head. "Out for a walk in the snow. Seems he's rarely seen this much snow but for a few times in his life."

"He should stay until February." Estelle rubbed her arms. "He'll have more snow than he wants."

"I still don't understand why he'd be all the way over here." Mama sighed. "Young people these days. They make me feel old."

"Yes, Mama, you are positively ancient." Catherine kissed her mother's cheek, then turned her attention to Dr. Rushmore. "What shall we do for him?"

"Let him rest. Keep him warm and watch for signs of fever. Call if he seems overly restless or flushed. I'll return tomorrow."

Mama rose. "I'll see you out, Doctor." She and Dr. Rushmore left the room.

Estelle faced Catherine and winked. "A rendezvous gone bad?"

"Not anything planned." Catherine snapped out the words.

Estelle laughed. "You just happened to find him in the snow? Isn't that too much of a coincidence?"

"We had no arrangement. I do, however, believe he must have been coming to see me. Otherwise, he would have stayed with the road or the shore."

"Curious." Estelle yawned. "We shall have to wait for the morning to find out."

But Catherine knew she couldn't sleep until she had some kind of an answer. If Tristram were at all up to talking, she intended to speak to him.

With Mama and Estelle back in their rooms, she told the footman on duty to wait in the corridor for a minute. Leaving the door open, she bent over Tristram. "You're not sleeping."

"You shouldn't be in here." His voice rose barely above a whisper.

"My mother is right across the hall and there's a footman who can see me if not hear me, so bear with me for a moment, please."

"Just one?" A ghost of a smile tipped up the corners of his mouth. "Not several?"

A tremor ran through her at his words, and she responded in a tone sharper than she intended. "I just need to know what you were doing on our lawn at half past ten o'clock at night."

"Coming to see you."

"Why?"

He started to shake his head, twisted his face in pain and raised his hands to press his palms against his temples. "Our bargain. I can call on you now. Miss Selkirk."

Disappointment leadened her stomach. He'd only come because of the bargain and the jewels, not a wish to see her after his trip into the city. She must stop this, control her disappointment—if she could. "It could have waited until morning." Annoyance with her foolish heart sharpened her tone.

"But you sent for me."

"I did not. I never would have."

"Of course you did. I was glad of the excuse to call."

"But— We'll talk tomorrow when you're rested." She started to step back.

He caught hold of her hand. "Wait." With surprising strength, he drew her closer. "Wait. I must tell you."

"Tomorrow."

"No, please." His grip, surprisingly strong, tightened. And his touch made her warm, tingling with current. "You know perfectly well." He took a deep breath. "I didn't fall and hit my head." He opened his eyes and held her gaze. "Someone hit me."

Catherine's hand jerked in his, but he didn't let go. She stared at him with wide eyes and her face paled. "You must be mistaken."

He started to shake his head, remembered how much

doing so hurt and chose to smile instead. "Not mistaken. I have been hit in the head before."

"But no one else was out in that weather."

"We were."

"Yes, but we're…" She looked away, and her cheeks turned the color of a ripe strawberry.

"Different from other people?"

They were two of a kind. And therein lay the words he could not say to her, the true reason why, the instant the snow ceased, he ignored the message telling him to call in the morning and headed down the hill to Lake House— he wanted to see her right then. Freed from the Selkirks' persistent round of activities, he longed for a moment with the Dowager Countess of Bisterne.

He'd received a far different reception than he anticipated. And he was a fool.

She drew her hand from his and her mouth tightened. "I'm not different from other people. I follow the rules now."

He laughed and raised his hand, but couldn't reach her cheek. "You wouldn't be here with me if that were true."

"I was looking in on you to see if you needed anything." She took a step back. "Do you wish me to call the police? They're right outside the gate."

"I have no enemies of which I am aware." He glanced at her from the corner of his eye. "Except for you."

"However you got that blow on your head, my lord, it seems to have scrambled your wits. Tell the footman if you need anything." Without bidding him good-night, she left the room.

Tristram watched her go and laughed to himself. She might think she was following the rules, but she harbored a rebellious heart, a spirit that didn't agree with society's strictures that insisted ladies do nothing of much good.

Wearing that mauve-and-green gown to the annual ball told him that the instant he set eyes on her.

"I know more about you than you think, my lady."

According to information Estelle had shared with Florian, who then told Tristram in some confusion that neither he nor any of his family knew, Catherine hadn't spent the four years of imprisonment at Bisterne doing nothing but complaining about her miserable life and choosing wallpaper for bedrooms. At least once a month, she had visited every family dependent on the estate. If they needed anything, she saw that they received it, paying for it from her own money.

Another motivation for taking the jewels, for wanting to stop him from proving her guilt? Perhaps when the earl died, leaving her no right to remain in the house her money had restored, she thought the family owed her something.

Or perhaps she was not guilty at all.

The conflicting messages in his head made his bruised brain hurt more. He longed for sleep. Yet the picture of Catherine in her plain gray suit, so proper, so prim, yet standing beside him holding his hand, made him restless.

He had to stop himself from saying her name aloud. Catherine, the name of so many queens throughout history, plain and simple yet regal. But nothing about Catherine was plain or simple. Nothing about his feelings for her was plain or simple. He adored her as much as he distrusted her.

"Lord, I want peace, not this constant turmoil."

"Sir? My lord?" The footman spoke from his chair across the room.

"Never mind. Just talking aloud, apparently."

"All right. I'm here if you need anything." The young man settled back in the soft chair.

Tristram again tried to sleep. He dozed some, only to wake with a start each time and again try to think up other options for how the jewels had gone missing. He grasped for others who might have bashed him on the head. And he failed at all.

Morning, and the arrival of Florian, came before sleep claimed him.

"What were you thinking, old man?" Florian drew the footman's abandoned chair closer to the bed and lounged against the winged back. "Wandering about in the dark and snow?"

"Walking about in the snow. It was a beautiful night."

"And what a convenient way to get into the lioness's den. Shall I nip down the hall and search her room?"

"While paying court to her sister? I think not."

Florian heaved an exaggerated sigh. "That's the rub of it, isn't it? She'll never have me if she finds out I've been helping you prove her sister is a jewel thief."

"I suppose there's an alternative." Tristram sat propped against pillows with a breakfast tray laid across his lap. Tea and buttered toast were all he could manage. He poured more of the former from a blue china pot. "Like proving she isn't a thief."

"What?" Florian shot upright. "What nonsense is this?"

"Probably nonsense," he said, turning the tea to acid and the toast to lead in his stomach.

"You can't possibly think she's innocent, can you?"

"I don't know what to think, but I'm no good lying here."

"I suppose you can't even talk to her."

Tristram said nothing of the midnight visit, nor his certainty that someone had struck him down. "I need to get back to the Selkirks'."

"Dr. Rushmore says not to move you for at least two days in this weather." Florian yawned and stretched. "Gives me an excellent excuse to come by and stay for hours."

"And spend your time with your young lady rather than your ailing friend." Tristram mock-scowled.

"She appreciates my company. You, I think, prefer some-one else's."

"Whose company could I possibly prefer?"

Florian laughed and departed.

Pierce followed an hour later, his face tight as a footman showed him into the sickroom, relaxing only once he was alone with Tristram.

"Managed not to see any of the VanDorn ladies, have you?" Tristram asked.

"Not today."

"She won't come in here," he added.

Pierce glanced around the room. "I didn't think I'd ever find myself in this house again."

"Which makes no sense. Don't you think the Lord wants you all to put this feud in the past? Ca— Lady Bisterne did something stupid, but it's over with."

"It won't be done with until Georgie marries." Pierce's long, narrow face grew even longer. "Her continued spin-sterhood is a constant reminder that her fiancé was stolen out from under her nose by a member of this household."

Another reminder of the chasm that lay between him and Catherine.

He crumbled a piece of toast. "I'll leave as soon as I can. Meanwhile, you needn't return."

"Oh, no, I need to keep an eye on Georgie's interests." Pierce laughed as though intending to make a joke, but no mirth rang through.

"I would like to see the feud end for all your sakes," Tristram said. "Carrying on the animosity hurts you all."

"You always were a benevolent fellow." Pierce rose and opened a leather case he had brought with him. "Brought you your Bible and some other books you had in your room." He laid the volumes on a bedside table easy to Tris-tram's hand. "And a chessboard, if you're not too concussed to play."

"You want to take advantage of me to finally win a game."

Pierce snorted. "It would be a fine change. But first I want you to tell me what you were doing out and about in the snow, and *here,* of all places."

Tristram shrugged, winced and laid his head back far enough that he was looking at the crown molding on the wall. "I like the snow, especially when it's fresh. As for here? Will you believe coincidence?"

"No. And neither will Georgette." Pierce removed the dishes from the breakfast tray and began to set up the chessboard. "You paid a late call on Catherine the instant you could get away from us. I'd like to say it is none of my business, but since my sister has decided she would like to be Lady Tristram, I'm a little concerned about your interest in the lovely widow."

Tristram was more than a little concerned about his interest in the lovely widow.

"I'll take white this time," he said by way of telling his friend he wouldn't discuss Catherine.

They began to play, but Tristram forgot half his moves and lost the first game far too quickly. Instead of concentrating on the game, Tristram thought about finding Catherine there when he gained consciousness, and further back, the thrill of receiving a message saying she wanted to see him. She didn't even know he'd gotten Georgette to visit, and Catherine asked him to call. Foolish of him to go dashing through the snow, but…

"You're not paying attention." Pierce began to pack up the chess set. "Mrs. VanDorn has told me by way of the butler that I may come anytime I like, so I'll leave you to rest and return later." He went to the door, but paused. "I'm not mentioning this incident to Georgette. She'll be on the next train running from the city and I don't think you want that right now."

Tristram rested after Pierce left, and woke with a dull throb in his head instead of crippling pain—an improvement. Sometime while he had slept, a footman had appeared. The man sprang up the moment Tristram opened his eyes and offered to fetch shaving water and fresh clothes.

"The ladies would like to see you, my lord. Can you walk as far as the conservatory?"

"I can."

It took him several minutes longer than the walk of forty feet should have, vertigo halting his steps. The view of snow-clad trees and a lake glazed with ice made the effort worth the journey.

As did the appearance of Catherine in the doorway.

She wore a dark blue dress trimmed in white lace around the high neck, and she carried a tray from which wafted the scent of chocolate. "My favorite snowy-day drink." She set the tray on the table. "Estelle will be here in a few minutes. She and Florian have some notion that you need soothing music to heal your head. But I asked her to wait so I can talk to you about last night." She hesitated a moment near him, then sat on the sofa cushion beside him. "If you don't mind."

She appeared so domestic, so calm, so lovely, he wanted to shove the distressing notion of her as a thief out of his head once and for all.

"I do not." On the contrary, he liked having her near more than he should. He turned to face her. "I haven't changed my mind about what I told you. Someone did strike me from behind."

"But who and why? And why have you told me and no one else?"

"How do you know I've told no one else?"

"Pierce Selkirk would have the police here thinking he could blame us for it."

"Which is why I didn't tell anyone."

"Again, why?"

He looked into her beautiful eyes and the answer caught in his throat. He swallowed and shook his head.

"Shall I pour some chocolate for you?" She reached for the tall silver pot.

"No, thank you. I feel bad enough accepting your hospitality under the circumstances."

"I think the Lord wants us to extend hospitality to those in need regardless of circumstances. Love our enemies and all." She forced out a laugh. "Not that you're my enemy yet, seeing as how you haven't announced to the world that you believe me to be a jewel thief."

"That's the problem at stake, though, my lady. It's a bit worse than I originally thought...." His eyes felt scorched.

"What could be worse than being accused of a crime you didn't commit?"

Tristram looked at her directly and said, "Being accused of *two* crimes."

Chapter 9

Since it is not likely that anyone would go around the world being deliberately offensive to others, it may be taken for granted that obnoxious behavior is either the fault of thoughtlessness or ignorance—and for the former there is no excuse.

Emily Price Post

For a moment, Catherine could barely comprehend what the man had said. And then, in a rush, it came to her and she sprang to her feet.

"Lord Tristram, are you suggesting that *I* am the one who struck you on the head?"

He looked her in the eyes, then turned away. "I considered it."

"You considered it? You thought, even for a moment, that I am capable of—of—" Catherine slid to her knees beside the sofa. A lifetime of training kept her back straight when she wanted to bow forward under the weight upon her shoulders. "If you weren't too injured to be traveling on these roads, I'd tell you to leave."

"And I would rather not abuse your hospitality." He sounded so sad, she levered herself back onto the sofa and faced him. He gazed down at his hands clasping his knees. "I have been wrestling with this for hours. To take your kindness and then think something so heinous is unconscionable. I had to say something to you."

Unable to remain near him any longer for fear he would see the tears pooling in her eyes, she shot to her feet and stalked across the room to the window, where she could see the tree that had broken his fall. No footprints remained. Snow had drifted into the impressions and the sun had glazed over the surface, making it appear like icing on a wedding cake. She rested her forehead on the cool glass. "I saved your life. If I hadn't come out there when I did, you would have frozen to death."

"Precisely. You went out there when you did."

"You think—" She couldn't breathe. Spots danced before her eyes, and she pressed a hand to her chest, gasping as though someone had knocked a fist into her solar plexus.

"I didn't send you a note." She managed to choke out the words. "Yet you think I did so to draw you here and hit you over the head?"

"It made more sense when I wasn't with you." He spoke from right behind her, and she jumped. He curved one hand around her shoulder. "I had to be honest with you, as I am about the fact that my hunt for the missing jewels always leads back to you."

"You being struck in the head and left to perish in the snow leads you back to me." Her voice sounded thick, as though her high-boned lace collar were too tight. "I suppose that would make sense from your side of the matter. But I know I'm innocent and think perhaps there's someone else leading everything back to me."

"Who?" His tone was soft, gentle, warm enough to melt the snow on the lawn below them. "Do you think I like suspecting, even for a moment, that a lady as kind and lovely and generous as you is capable of harming me?"

"You think I'm capable of theft." Her words merely

rasped past her lips though she wanted them to emerge with force.

"Can you give me evidence to prove me wrong?" He used a fingertip to gather tears from beneath her eyes, then curved his hand around her cheek and turned her face toward him. "Please?"

"I don't know how." Through a veil of more tears, she gazed into his beautiful green eyes. Her mouth went dry. "You can't possibly want to…to…"

But he could. He did. He smoothed his hand down her cheek to her chin, tilted it up and kissed her.

She was a widow, and yet in that moment, she doubted she had ever been kissed, not with such tender warmth. Her knees wobbled, and she grasped his lapels for support. She inhaled his scent, and tasted bergamot and orange picot, and when he raised his head, she read wonder and confusion in his face. He blinked, gave his head a quick shake and flicked his glance from her to the windows and back.

His lips parted, and she braced herself for the humiliation of his apology, his words of regret.

"I probably shouldn't have done that?" It sounded more like a query than a statement.

"It's rather improper."

"Rather." He shoved his hands into his coat pockets and looked past her again.

She drew her brows together and sighed. "Just say it, Lord Tristram. You're sorry you kissed me. You regret forgetting that I'm a lady and therefore untouchable." She forced a smile to her lips. "All right, then. Apology accepted. Now may we get back to the business at hand?"

"No, I do not think we can." He brushed a wisp of hair from her cheek. "My lady—Catherine—I regret a number of interactions in our brief acquaintance. I regret having to investigate you. I regret thinking for one second you were behind the incident last night. But I do not regret kissing you."

If a woman could fall in love in so short a time as they had known one another, then she fell in love in that moment. Even the idea of it robbed her of speech, of coherent thought. She wanted to wrap her arms around him and rest her head on his shoulder. She wanted to have him hold her and assure her they would find the person truly guilty. She wanted him to take her home, despite the fact that home, to him, was another English manor.

Estelle bursting into the conservatory with her banjo tucked under one arm kept Catherine from doing anything more stupid than she already had when she'd let him kiss her.

"I'm sorry I kept you all waiting, but Florian sent around a message asking…" Estelle trailed off and glanced from Tristram to Catherine then back again, before grinning. "Did I interrupt something?"

"Nothing that cannot be renewed later." Tristram bowed. "How do you do, Miss VanDorn?"

"Quite well, thank you, but you look rather wobbly. Perhaps you should sit down."

"If you ladies will join me." He stepped back so Catherine could precede him.

Cheeks too warm to escape Estelle's notice, Catherine stumbled back to the sofa and collapsed onto the cushions. She picked up the teapot to pour, felt it tremble in her hand and set it down again. "Will you do the honors, Estelle? You need practice."

"So do you." Estelle was practically choking on suppressed laughter. It danced in her eyes and emerged as little coughs and sharp caught breaths. "Milk? You don't need sugar."

"Are you going to entertain us?" Catherine demanded more than asked.

"I will." Estelle set a cup in front of Tristram. "So what brought you out in a snowstorm?"

Tristram settled beside Catherine, keeping a proper six inches away. "The end of the storm. I needed fresh air after nearly a week in the city."

"But Florian says you work in the city—in London, that is." Estelle settled on the seat adjacent to Tristram.

"You work?" Catherine posed the question before she realized how foolish she sounded.

She had let him kiss her—she had kissed him back—and she knew so little about him. It wasn't the sort of behavior Mama had instilled in her. It was the sort of behavior that had given her a reputation for being fast and landed her in an English prison called a manor house.

"I don't know if I would call it work." Tristram shrugged off the subject. "A few other former officers and I work with men who were wounded in the Boer War and the Boxer Rebellion, and help them find work, get their pensions, learn new trades if they can't do the old ones. Most of them end up in the London stews, so that's where we go."

"How kind of you." Catherine gazed at him in awe. "I wish I'd known you when I was in England. I could have helped you raise money. I'm getting quite adept at organizing charity events."

"This operation is rather new, and my father has been generous." He ducked his head, but failed to hide the flush of color along his cheekbones. "I expect to make up for my failure as an officer."

"That's not what I heard it was." Estelle exchanged her teacup for the banjo she had tucked behind her chair, and began to pluck idly at the strings. "Ambrose told me—"

"A great deal of balderdash, I expect." Tristram raised a hand to the cowlick on his head, right above where he had been struck the night before.

"Estelle," Catherine said in haste, "why don't you entertain us from farther away. You tend to get a little loud."

"Especially once Florian gets here." She rose, still playing, and strolled to another grouping of chairs on the other side of the room.

Catherine touched Tristram's arm. "Do you need to return to your room?"

"Not yet." He clasped her hand and, still holding her fingers, lowered it to the cushion between them. "We need to talk."

"We do." Her fingers trembled beneath his. "Your father will take away the funds to your charity if you don't find the jewel thief."

"Yes, and more. Even if I inherit, if my brother's widow bears another girl, Father will give her all the money and property not entailed to the title. I will have an enormous estate to run without the money to run it."

"How irresponsible of him."

"Indeed." He tried to flatten his cowlick again but it sprang back into a tiny corkscrew curl Catherine fought not to reach up and smooth herself. "I can guess how many people that is."

"Nearly a hundred people potentially punished because my father is so ashamed of me he can see nothing but how to hurt me."

"Why such antagonism toward you? I mean, surely you couldn't have done anything too terrible in South Africa."

"In my role as a military officer I did. And my behavior as an officer is all that matters to my father. He's willing to damage his family lands and my charity work in order to show the world he doesn't tolerate me, either."

"That's horrible." She ached for him, but she ached for herself as well and extracted her hand from his hold. "Thus you need an heiress."

"It's not like that, Catherine. If you think that's why I kissed you, you're wrong."

"You thought you could lure me into revealing my secrets?"

"I thought I could do something I've wanted to do since you walked into that ballroom and ruffled feathers with that dress. You were so reckless, so defiant, so scared, I wanted to know your secrets."

"If only I had some to tell." She crossed her arms. "I don't. Everyone knows my husband neglected me. Everyone knows that old Mrs. Selkirk has convinced society that I, and thus my family, am too immoral for the good people of the Tuxedo Club to receive."

"She hasn't been particularly successful."

"This is a small enough community that that little is enough to hurt Mama and bar Estelle from certain gatherings where she should be seen."

"I do not think she cares."

Estelle perched on a chair with her head tilted back, her eyes closed and her fingers moving over the strings in a blur. She looked anything but distressed that she wasn't the belle of the season her elder sister had been.

"She saw how little good it has done me." Catherine fumbled in the pocket of her skirt for a handkerchief. It was black-bordered, as were all her handkerchiefs. Sapphire had sewn the edges upon Bisterne's death and Catherine hadn't purchased more.

Before she touched it to her eyes, Tristram took it from her and exchanged it for a larger linen square, plain white save for his initials in the same green as his eyes—*TBW.*

"Black doesn't suit you." He tucked her handkerchief into his coat pocket.

Catherine dabbed at her eyes. "What is the *B* for?"

"Baston-Ward."

Catherine spun around to face him again. "You're Florian's cousin?"

"And yours, by marriage. Very distantly."

"So there's more to this jewel-hunting than your father's old friend needing aid."

"It's my mother's family. Whatever else one might say about my father, he loved my mother. He's been different since she died, less patient, less forgiving of human frailty, which I, according to him, have in an overabundance."

"Because you chose to leave the army?"

"No, my dear. I didn't decide to leave. I disliked the service, but it was my duty as the second son, so I took it. I ended up in South Africa and…I was allowed to leave rather than be court-martialed."

Her face paled, and Tristram suppressed a twisted smile. He was used to that action of withdrawal, polite remoteness. A man wounded and leaving the military because of it was one thing. One allowed to resign his commission out of respect for his father's title and the number of Wolfes and Baston-Wards who had served before him, was quite something else. A court-martial would have meant he had let his country down.

She would regret kissing him now, if she didn't already. Her remark about him needing an heiress made that clear, though only moments earlier, she had looked utterly besotted—the way he felt. It had distracted them both from the thoughtless way he'd accused her of bashing him over the head in the snow. He shouldn't have spoken that suspicion aloud. The evidence was only circumstantial.

All the evidence against her was circumstantial. Besides, she cared about him. She had learned how to control her outward expression of emotions well, but not perfectly. Even as she lashed back at his accusations, she looked hurt, not angry. It was longing he saw in her eyes, not contempt.

Until now. The blow on his head must have weakened him enough to tell her the truth. Or perhaps it was giving in to the desire to kiss her that had loosened his tongue. It was a gamble, and her face told him it was not a gamble that would pay off.

"Insubordination, not cowardice." He may as well get it all out. "It was a horrible, unnecessary and unjust war and I despised my superior officers for how they were treating the people of the country. They herded them into camps like animals. Sheep ready for the slaughter were treated better. So I refused to destroy the village I was ordered to subdue and let the people escape to safety. One of them thanked me with a blow to the head, which truly was a gift. It gave the army a reason to let me resign."

The liquid notes of Estelle's banjo filled in the silence like water seeking a channel between two rocks. Catherine stared at him with those wide eyes that made him want to drown in their velvety depths. His mouth dry, he reached for his tea, now cold with a skim of milk clouding the surface.

"Don't drink that. I'll ring for more." She jumped up so quickly electricity crackled from her wool skirt against the velvet cushion.

He reached out with some notion of stopping her, but let his hand fall. If she wanted to use tea as an excuse to get away from him, the disgraced officer, than he would not stop her.

She rang the bell. As she gave her orders to the footman who appeared, the doorbell chimed.

Estelle stopped playing mid arpeggio and sprang to her feet. "Florian is here."

Tristram glanced at her face, glowing as though electric lights burned behind it, and felt a groan rise in his chest. She had fallen for Florian, who possessed no prospects and less money without the jewels. That Estelle was an heiress made the situation worse. Her parents would never approve after Catherine's experience.

He needed to find the jewels and get Florian back to England and out of harm's way—or rather, keep Estelle out of harm's way. Yet how could he continue to call on Catherine if she now rejected him?

He turned just as Florian came into view with Ambrose right behind him.

"Look what the cat dragged in." Florian gestured behind him. "A veritable throng to comfort you, Tris."

He wasn't gesturing solely at Ambrose. Two more people reached the point where the steps opened into the conservatory.

Pierce and Georgette Selkirk.

Chapter 10

The custom of raising the hat when meeting an acquaintance derives from the old rule that friendly knights in accosting each other should raise the visor for mutual recognition in amity. In the knightly years, it must be remembered, it was important to know whether one was meeting friend or foe. Meeting a foe meant fighting on the spot. Thus, it is evident that the conventions of courtesy not only tend to make the wheels of life run more smoothly, but also act as safeguards in human relationship.

Emily Price Post

The sight of Georgette—as bright as the sunshine melting snow from the roof—sent a shock wave of guilt racing through Catherine. Here she was ready to beg forgiveness for the past, a goal she had striven for nearly since she left America, and yet she had kissed one more of Georgette's beaux not a half hour ago. Given warning of Georgette's arrival, she might have run away to hide her shame.

Instead, she stepped forward to extend her hands in welcome. "You chose a cold day for making calls." Not an auspicious greeting. "I mean… That is—"

Georgette interrupted with her sparkling laughter. "We just got back from the city, and I needed a guarantee that neither Mama nor Grandmama would want to stir from the drawing room fire."

The two of them stood a dozen feet apart, eyeing one another, while the others watched the tableau unfold. Georgette looked as young and golden as she had five years earlier. Her complexion and hair glowed in the lamplight. Her well-cut gown emphasized the lithe lines of her form. Best of all, her smile was as wide and warm as it had been all their years of friendship.

Wishing she were wearing something finer than a dark gray walking suit with only the narrowest bands of lace to adorn her collar, Catherine took the first step forward. Georgette mirrored her actions. They met in the center of the Persian carpet to hug, neither speaking, neither moving. Tears pooled in Catherine's eyes. Georgette had come to her when she was the wronged party. She tried to say something appropriate to the moment, but her voice would not come, blocked by too many words she had considered saying over the past five years.

In the doorway, a footman gave a discreet cough.

Catherine stepped back, indicating the need for fresh coffee services on the low table between the sofas. The servant's presence gave Catherine time to compose herself and dab at her eyes with her handkerchief—no, Tristram's handkerchief. When she pulled the linen away, Georgette was seated facing the lake, where Tristram had been. He had joined the others on the other side of the room. Estelle reigned there, dispensing coffee and tea and making everyone laugh.

Georgette perched on the edge of the cushion, her cheeks damp but her smile firmly in place. "I always loved this room."

"It's my favorite." Catherine took up the coffeepot. "Though I suppose I should have asked if you prefer tea now."

"Coffee. But no sugar. I get plump if I'm not careful."

Catherine smiled. "I find that difficult to believe."

"It's true. If I didn't walk miles a day on these hills or play tennis, I would look like a snowball in a white dress." Georgette accepted the coffee cup with its generous dollop of cream. "I rather overindulged myself with sweets after…" She trailed off. Her gaze flicked to Catherine, then down to her coffee.

"After I eloped with your fiancé?" Catherine opened the door as wide as it could go. Her hands shook, and she left her cup on its saucer.

Across the room, Florian was trying to play Estelle's banjo, while the others groaned and laughed.

Catherine took a deep breath and plunged in. "Georgette, this is still likely not enough to make up for the humiliation and pain I caused you and your family, and I have to tell you that he wasn't worth a moment of your grief. He wanted nothing more than the money. He wasn't the least interested in me once that ring was on my finger and my dowry in his bank account."

"So I heard." Georgette turned her blue eyes fully on Catherine. "People from here visited London and sometimes saw him. Apparently he acted as though he barely remembered your name." She set her cup on the table and leaned forward. "At first, I thought it was the least you deserved. I couldn't bear to go out in public for weeks because I hated the sympathetic looks. And a few young men…" Her cheeks flushed. "They thought they could take advantage of my jilted state, if you understand what I'm saying."

"I do. I encountered those same sort after I was widowed."

They exchanged sympathetic glances, a fragile camaraderie starting to take hold.

"He took me to that moldering old house of his," Catherine continued, "then left for London, where he stayed most of the time." She plucked at the smooth wool of her skirt. "But all that doesn't make up for what I did to you in luring him away. And I, well, I beg your forgiveness for putting such a shallow desire for a title before our friendship."

Speech delivered, Catherine sagged back against the sofa cushions and waited for a sense of relief, of the peace that had eluded her for over five years. Instead, she felt worse than she had before.

Lord Tristram's voice, clear and smooth, though no louder than the others, rang through her head, winding her insides like a seven-day clock. Her apology to her friend meant almost nothing, because of what she'd allowed to happen with him.

Georgette remained silent. So silent, the conversation of the others began to falter. Then, when Florian's inexpert plucking of the banjo strings was the only sound in the conservatory, she grasped the silver tongs, dropped a lump of sugar into her coffee and began to stir. "Carry on." She spoke without looking at the others.

They burst into a cacophony of conversation.

Georgette fixed her attention on Catherine. "At first, I hated you. I rather hoped your ship would sink in the middle of the Atlantic."

Catherine flinched, but wasn't truly surprised. She expected she would have felt the same in reverse.

"Then when I heard all wasn't like a fairy tale for you," Georgette continued, "I thought it was what you deserved and thought if he'd married me, he wouldn't have treated me that way. Rather arrogant of me, isn't it?" She laughed, sipped some of her coffee and grimaced. "Why did I put sugar in this?"

"Old habit?"

"Bad habit." Georgette nudged her cup toward the center of the table. "I forgive you, Catherine. I forgave you a long time ago. At first it was just what I knew was the right thing to do, and then it was genuine, what I knew the Lord wanted from me."

"Thank you. But why—Georgette, I have to ask—why have you never married? Surely you haven't been pining for Edwin."

"Not Edwin. A man who will take me away from all this." She swept her arm in an arc. "I am so weary of seeing the same people at the same parties year after year. When I go into the city, I want to attend the less savory theaters, those productions the immigrants put on. I want to go to Coney Island in the summer and take a boat from the city to Lake Erie. Lord Bisterne represented all that to me. He would take me away to another world." For a moment, her eyes shimmered like a summer sky, then the light died. "But I'm stranded here in Tuxedo Park most of the time with a mother and grandmother who are more bitter over my broken engagement than I ever was."

Catherine sighed on behalf of her friend. "What will change things?"

"Perhaps if I marry another title?" A half smile played around Georgette's lips.

Catherine knew instantly to whom her friend was referring, and her heart sank.

Surely if she truly wanted to mend fences between the families and stop old Mrs. Selkirk's vicious tongue, Catherine would be happy for Georgette. She and Tristram seemed to be getting along well. But an elephant seemed to be sitting on her chest.

"Should I be congratulating you?" she asked.

Should she scorn him for kissing her while Georgette believed they had an unofficial understanding?

Across the room, he now held the banjo and Estelle was showing him how to position his fingers.

"If you played any instrument at all," she was saying, "this might be easier."

"He used to play the piano," Florian said.

Just one more thing Catherine didn't know about him.

Eyes lowered, Georgette leaned toward Catherine. "It's a little too soon, but I do have expectations. He is handsome and kind and, most of all, interesting."

"Yes, quite," Catherine murmured.

"Back in England," Georgette continued, "he works to help men wounded in those two wars the English have been involved in lately. Something like the Boer War in China?"

"South Africa. China was the Boxer Rebellion."

Georgette shrugged off details. "Lots of men come home wounded and don't have a way to support themselves other than small pensions. Some don't even have homes, so he and other former military men raise money to help them learn trades or get back to their old ones."

"So I understand."

"He won't say, but I think he's come over here to raise money for his cause because his father might not give him his inheritance."

So Georgette suspected the same of him as Catherine did. Had he kissed Georgette as well, to ensure he caught at least one heiress?

"I don't know any details," Georgette continued, "but there is something about him having incomplete business and his father being angry with him for leaving the military service."

So she didn't know about the court-martial.

"I should think it's his duty to his country to serve," Georgette said, "but he was wounded, so perhaps that makes continuing to serve difficult. It doesn't matter since if he marries an heiress, he won't need to concern himself with a bit of money from his father. Marrying to help dozens or hundreds of men recover from the war is so much more noble than merely restoring an old house."

"Indeed it is." Catherine glanced out the windows to

where the wind was whipping the tree branches into a fury and clouds quickly replaced the blue sky. The lake lay still and flat beneath its layer of ice as snow began to fall.

Catherine suddenly longed to be out there chasing those flakes with the wind yanking back her hood and tugging the pins from her hair. She wanted to howl with the elements even though she was getting what she wanted—a renewal of friendship with Georgette, which was the first step to reconciliation between their families. She should be ecstatic. She wanted to weep over how she couldn't continue a dull existence in Tuxedo Park knowing Georgette was in England with Tristram, working at his side, loving him...

Catherine moved to the sofa beside Georgette and they began to fill in details of the missing years between them. Georgette wanted to know all about life in an English country house, and in Europe. Catherine acknowledged that her life hadn't been complete misery. She had acres of garden to restore and running her own household was rewarding. European society was generally dull, but the sights were spectacular.

Georgette filled her in on details about their school friends. "Susan Lassiter went to college, if you can believe it," Georgette confided. "Someplace in Ohio. Oberlin, that was it. She is now studying to be a doctor at Johns Hopkins in Baltimore."

"That's astounding. Her parents let her?"

"She inherited money from her grandfather and her parents couldn't stop her. But they sold their house here in the Park right after she left and spend their summers in Bar Harbor and winters in Boston. I think they're ashamed of her."

"I'd be proud of my daughter for elevating herself above shallow pursuits."

Catherine wondered about her own life, spending her days doing nothing more than planning what to wear to the next social gathering, trying to keep Estelle from thinking about running off to join a band or Ambrose or Florian, or sitting by a fire with her needlework while others gossiped around her. Once she wanted nothing more than to be the most popular girl at a ball and to marry a title. Once she got those, she realized she needed more, if only she knew then what that was.

She knew now. She needed Tristram, meaningful work like his charity, the freedom to care about him without ruining relationships between the Selkirks and VanDorns again.

"Susan wants to be a missionary," Georgette said. "She writes to me now and again, and sometimes I am inspired to seek something more than this life we are so privileged to have. But now that I've met Lord Tristram, well…" She laughed. "I've decided perhaps that is where the Lord wants me to serve others—at his side in the London slums."

"That's noble of you. I helped nurse some of the children on the estate a few years ago when there was a measles outbreak. It was exhausting, but rewarding."

"Perhaps we could work on something together, beginning with your mother's annual tea. We will buy a ticket and come this year. I'll make Pierce and Tristram come, as well. And for now…" Georgette rose. "I had better go home before the weather gets any worse. Grandmother predicted this, which is why we came home today. With Lord Tristram out here, she didn't want me stranded in the city." She glanced his way and blushed.

Catherine looked away, her face as cold as Georgette's looked warm. "Thank you for coming." She couldn't look at her old friend. "I don't deserve your forgiveness."

"Of course you do. I would be in the wrong if I didn't give it."

They embraced again, and Georgette departed with her brother and admonitions to the Englishmen not to tarry and get stranded. Pierce was too polite not to bow to Catherine, but it was little more than an inclination of his head. He, apparently, was not ready to put the past behind him.

Ignoring the protests of the Englishmen and Estelle, Catherine crossed to the windows and flung open one of the casements to feel the blast of icy air in her face in lieu of a walk.

Despite Tristram's maintaining his part of their bargain, she couldn't uphold hers. Georgette wanted him, and Catherine couldn't risk damaging that friendship and the potential for softening the hearts of the older Selkirk ladies by the appearance of Tristram paying her particular attention. At the same time, if she couldn't see him and convince him of her innocence, her name might never be cleared and her family would suffer.

"What do I do, Lord?" she cried out the prayer that had been in her heart for years.

And as had happened for years, she received no response. Worse, when she closed the window and faced the room, she met Tristram's eyes, and her knees nearly buckled beneath her.

This, then, was her answer—she could have peace and friendship with Georgette, which would benefit her entire family, or she could explore a future with Tristram and convince him of her innocence along the way, which would also benefit her family.

And potentially give her a broken heart, if he were merely wooing her to gain a measure of his father's respect.

She owed Georgette too much to risk hurting her again. She had already cost her friend Lord Bisterne, who might not have been a terrible husband to Georgette. Perhaps her lively effervescence was what he needed to hold his interest. Perhaps Georgette could have kept him at home and thus kept him alive.

Heart pounding against the painful tightness in her

chest, Catherine headed for the steps without looking at the others.

Tristram caught her hand as she passed. "You aren't going to join us, my lady?"

"No." She drew her hand free before the contact sent her heart racing even harder. "I must work on the charity ball."

She turned her back on him and left the room.

Chapter 11

A young man walking with a young woman should be careful that his manner in no way draws attention to her or to himself. Too devoted a manner is always conspicuous, and so is loud talking. Under no circumstances should he take her arm, or grasp her by or above the elbow, and shove her here and there, unless, of course, to save her from being run over!

Emily Price Post

Tristram had not seen her alone since his return to the Selkirks. He had called on her—twice. Both times, she was not at home, though he knew perfectly well that she was.

He never should have told her about the court-martial. At the time, once she recovered from her initial shock, she seemed sympathetic, completely understanding of his actions. But perhaps he'd misread her. She had walked out of the conservatory without talking to him again. And she had stayed away from him until Dr. Rushmore freed him to go home the following day.

She was fully occupied helping ladies plan their charity events. One even took her into the city for a few days. Yet when she returned, she spent her time with Georgette. Georgette had called on Catherine three times in the intervening days.

"It's so wonderful to have her friendship again. I have missed her." It was all Georgette said to him about Catherine.

"I don't know if Georgie can trust her," Pierce confided in Tristram. "Even if the man turned out to be a scoundrel, Georgie still broke her heart over Lord Bisterne."

Georgette was going to break her heart over him, too, Tristram feared. He didn't love her. He didn't even think he could love her in a mutually beneficial arrangement, at least as nothing more than the deep affection one feels for a friend. Yet he was surrounded by her brother and father and his own compatriots, who told him at least once a day he should offer for the pretty heiress.

The problem, of course, was Catherine. He had kissed her, and the very memory of it shocked him, that he had kissed her and she responded in a favorable manner. After contact like that, he should be able to trust her, but he didn't. She had broken her word. Not giving him an opportunity to call on her once he arranged matters with Georgette renewed his assurance that she was not being honest about the jewels.

Yet having kissed Catherine, he found no interest in a deep relationship with Georgette.

What message God was trying to give him escaped his comprehension. To give up on the jewel hunt? Surely not. To marry Georgette, who had all the right qualities for his wife, though he couldn't bring himself to have the right sort of feelings for her? Also unlikely. To seek elsewhere for the jewel thief? He didn't know where to look.

"If you married an heiress," Ambrose pointed out one day when he, Florian and Tristram were alone in one of the Selkirks' parlors, you could pay the Baston-Wards for the jewels and appease your father."

"Even if that would make my father happy, which I doubt, I'd rather find other reasons for marrying a lady, heiress or not." Catherine's lovely face haunted his mind's eye. He shoved the image away.

He couldn't make an offer for Catherine.

Then you shouldn't have kissed her, the reprimand sounded in his head.

"I'd marry an heiress if I had a title or even a fine house in England to exchange for her dowry." Ambrose sounded anguished. The father of his textile heiress in New York refused him calling privileges. Two steps from a title was two steps too far for even a minor millionaire to find acceptable. "These Americans are such odd sticklers."

Florian's mouth curled in a smile. "I will marry an heiress without my own fine house or title."

"You won't, if her parents don't approve." A gleam entered Ambrose's eyes, as though he relished Florian being as unhappy as he was. "You wouldn't get her fine dowry."

"Then we shall live on our wits and music." Florian's calm assurance was naive and rather refreshing in this world driven by a man's bank account.

"You're a fool for not taking advantage of Georgette's adoration of you," Ambrose declared to Tristram.

"Perhaps I—" A knock on the parlor door interrupted Tristram.

A footman entered bearing a silver tray containing a yellow envelope. "Telegram for you, my lord."

Tristram felt as though he had swallowed a snowball whole, as he took the telegram and pulled the flimsy sheet of paper from the envelope.

You are wasting your time stop Thought you could at least succeed in this simple task stop Home by first of year regardless stop

Tristram didn't want to be a failure. He wanted to prove his father wrong about him, if just once. He doubted going home with an heiress wife would improve his father's opinion of him. And the marquess would consider that cheating.

So he tried to find other ways to see Catherine and glean information from her, catching her where she could not avoid him. Unfortunately, she attended few of the same social gatherings to which the Selkirks accepted invitations. Even then she stayed with her own circle of friends. But one day, needing a view outside the fence, he walked into the village. It was small and efficiently built—thoroughly built despite having been put up in mere months some fifteen years earlier, which gave it a homogeneous feel. Still, the change of scenery and the sight of ordinary people going about their work refreshed his spirits.

Then, wanting some peppermints, he entered the chemist—or rather, the drugstore, as the Americans called it—and saw Estelle.

He bowed to her and murmured a greeting.

"Good day, Lord Tristram." She wrapped her arm around her collected shopping as though hiding the intended purchases. "Odd to see you in the village."

"And you. I didn't know young ladies from the Park purchased their own ordinary things."

"Some of us do. Catherine has always—" She stopped and narrowed her eyes.

"Catherine would." With nothing to lose except perhaps some pride, he asked, "Where has she been of late? She's never home to me."

Estelle shrugged. "She's good at keeping herself occupied from dawn to dusk. Shall I pass a message along for you?"

"No, thank you." Tristram hesitated, then added, "Actually, if you wouldn't mind, just tell her I will see her at the tea, if not sooner."

To everyone's shock, all the Selkirk ladies had decided to attend the charitable event. Ambrose and Florian were part of the genteel entertainment, and Pierce and Tristram intended to accompany the ladies. But though Tristram felt that the tea was not a good prospect for private conversation with Catherine, and he was anxious to speak with her as soon as possible, he didn't see her again until the evening of Thanksgiving Day.

He, like many of the Tuxedo Park residents, had made his way to the clubhouse to recover from an abundant dinner. Half dozing from the heat of the fire on the great hearth, he started upright at a blast of cold swirling from the front door opening. He glanced that way and saw a lady's skirt flouncing through the opening. A moment later, she flitted past the window, tall and graceful even tramping through the snow.

Catherine.

He excused himself to the gentlemen with whom he had been engaged in desultory conversation, snatched up his coat, hat and gloves, and strode after the lady.

Finding her path proved simple. Her small feet had left deep impressions in the snow, blurred from where her skirt swirled around her. The lady had foolishly chosen to cut a trail through the untouched snow along the woodland path rather than take the road. Tuxedo Park might be as safe as one's own garden, but she still shouldn't be out alone at night. Of course, she might have caught a glimpse of him on her way out of the clubhouse and was trying to avoid him by cutting a trail of her own.

"No such fortune, my lady," Tristram said. His mouth set, he followed the footprints, making no effort to quiet the crunch of his bootheels on the snow's glazed surface or fallen branches. He wanted to talk to her, not sneak up behind her and terrify her.

His strides longer than hers, he soon caught a glimpse of her, a graceful figure in dark wraps taking measured steps in the as yet untouched whiteness. She had to have heard him, but she neither sped up nor slowed.

At last, he closed the distance between them and slipped his hand beneath her elbow. "Did you think you could avoid me forever in a closed community like this one?"

"I intended to give it a valiant attempt." She removed her arm from his hold. "I still do."

"Even though that means breaking your word?"

She said nothing. Starlight blazing through the bare tree branches sparkled on the frosty breath that issued from between her pursed lips. Temperatures ranged well below freezing, bringing to mind how warm her lips could be, had been, should be.

He jerked his gaze away to the dim path before them. "You told me you would be at home to me if I persuaded Georgette to mend fences. Now the whole family is coming to your charity tea. I more than upheld my end of the bargain. Now it is your turn."

"I can't see you." She recommended walking. "I made that promise before I knew that Georgette…" She raised her hands to draw the fur-edged hood of her coat around her face. Tristram took her elbow again.

"I know about Georgette's plans." He tucked her arm against his side. The action warmed him, though he hesitated to examine why.

She tensed as though intending to pull away again, but did not. "Do you not mean her feelings for you?"

"I say what I mean. You should know that by now."

"Touché." She let out a laugh. "You keep your word while I do not. But surely you don't hold that against me."

"Dishonest in one thing, likely dishonest in others."

She tried to pull her arm away but he would not let her.

The trees broke at a meadow, and he turned to face her. "I want to believe you, Catherine, but you are not helping me as you said you would."

"I cannot." Frustration tinged her voice. "I can't risk Georgette thinking I am trying to take you away from her."

"You cannot take from her what she does not have."

"She doesn't know that she does not have you. She believes you—" She shook her head. "I can't betray a confidence more than I already have."

"It's no confidence." He tilted his head back and sighed, forming a cloud between himself and the heavens. "She thinks I'm hers for the asking. She looks at me like I will turn up wrapped in shiny paper and tucked under the Christmas tree. And if I disillusion her, I will no longer be welcome at Tuxedo Park, where the trail of the missing jewels led me."

"And you're convinced it's not a false trail?"

"The jewels are real enough."

"I expect the ones sold to jewelers are real enough. Perhaps only the ones given to *me* were artificial." She sighed. "I should have noticed. I never suspected Edwin to be so... so stingy."

"If he even knew."

She gave him a quick, sharp glance. "What do you mean?"

"How much did he interact with the jewels?"

Her shoulders moved, pressing her arm into his side in a way that thrilled through him. "I never saw him take them out of the safe. He only went into the safe on one of the quarter days to safeguard the rents until the next time he went to the bank."

"Which was when?"

"Michaelmas last year."

"And the jewels were there then?"

"I saw them. He opened all the cases and looked at them as usual. He asked me—" A noise somewhere between a gasp and a sob caught at her voice. "He asked me if I had any parties to which I wanted to wear any of them. Then he laughed and closed up the safe. Later that day, he took the train up to London, and the next day, Ambrose took it down to Bisterne to tell me Edwin was...gone."

"I'm sorry." Tristram freed her arm from where he'd tucked it against his side, and took her hand. He curled his fingers around hers as securely as he could with both of them wearing gloves. "I knew Edwin was neglectful of you. I didn't know he was cruel."

"God is working on my heart to forgive him. And myself." Her voice dropped to a near whisper, but the woods lay in such stillness Tristram heard her.

"Forgiving isn't always easy."

"No, but Georgette forgave me for how I hurt her. That has helped me see my way clear to not hanging on to my bitterness against my husband." Her fingers moved restlessly in his hand, though she made no attempt to draw away. "I owe her for that on top of everything else."

"You owe her nothing, Catherine. Forgiveness is her responsibility. And as for the fiancé, Bisterne is the one who broke a promise, not you."

"Then why doesn't society see it that way?" Suddenly, she stooped, and came up with both hands full of snow. She formed the snow into a ball and threw it against the nearest tree as hard as she could. The snow missile exploded in a puff of white, and she quickly followed it with another and another to emphasize her words. "My family has been shunned by several hostesses. I have to endure old Mrs. Selkirk telling me with whom I can and cannot associate. And I dare not disobey for all I'm twenty-four." She was throwing the balls of snow so rapidly now that Tristram began to laugh, in awe of her. "And a widow. And my trust fund can buy and sell the Selkirks twice over. And if you don't stop laughing, I will—"

The final snowball struck him squarely on the chin. Snow filled his mouth, shot up his nose and managed to slip between his muffler and neck. Shock of the impact knocked him back a step. He slipped in the white stuff and ended up sitting in the snow, still laughing.

"Are you all right?" Catherine dropped to her knees beside him. "I didn't mean to— I never should have—" She raised her hand to his face and brushed away the snow.

He caught hold of her fingers and held them to his cheek, as warm inside as the snow was cold outside. "It's quite all right, my dear. But if it's a snowball fight you want, give me the opportunity to arm myself and make it fair."

She backed away. "I don't think that would be proper for a dowager countess."

"Nor is walking through the woods alone at night, but you were doing it." He gathered snow as he scrambled to his feet. "Nor do they throw snowballs at the sons of peers, yet you did." On the last word, he lobbed the packed snow at her, aiming for her shoulder.

It struck just high enough to knock back her hood and send snow sliding beneath her collar. She shrieked, grabbed snow from the top of a drift and shot it back.

And the battle was on. To Tristram's chagrin, Catherine was a better shot than he was. What he lacked in accuracy, he made up for in speed. He kept her darting from tree to tree.

Finally she collapsed against one, her hands on her knees, where snow encrusted her gown, her breaths rushing in and out of her lungs. "Uncle. Uncle."

He'd never heard the expression, but got the message. Out of breath himself, he closed the distance between them and took her hands to lift her upright. "I didn't hurt you, did I?"

"Only my pride that I had to surrender." She tilted her head back. Her face glowed in the starlight, and her eyes danced with laughter.

He wanted to kiss her. Oh, how he wanted to enjoy a

second embrace there in that quiet clearing. No one would interrupt them there.

Which was precisely why he had to let her go. He had no right to touch her, to disrespect her, because they were alone and had already enjoyed a quarter hour of play.

"Let me take you home." His voice was a mere rasp.

She nodded and tucked her hand into the crook of his elbow all on her own this time. They headed out in silence save for the rhythmic crunching of their footfalls, yet the lack of conversation felt comfortable, companionable. Shared laughter was a powerful bond—so powerful a bond, he feared he could too easily love her.

Perhaps he already did.

That thought made him feel colder than the night air. He dared not love her. Caring for her even a little had already clouded his perspective where her guilt was concerned. Loving her would destroy his will to learn the truth at all.

He marshaled the words he must speak to her before bidding her good-night, and was ready with them when they reached her front door. "You will be at home the next time I call." He delivered the sentence without the hint of a query in his pitch. It was a statement, almost a command.

She drew her hand from his arm. "I cannot. Even tonight was disloyal to Georgette."

Her loyalty to her friend pushed him a little closer to the edge of falling in love. "I have made no promises to Georgette. I made a promise to you in exchange for you making yourself available when I call. Monday, she and her mother are going to some debutante's tea party." They reached her front steps. "You're safely home. And you will be here at two o'clock on Monday."

She sighed. "All right."

"Thank you." He indulged himself with the merest

brush of his lips on her cheek, then waited for the butler to let her into the house before he strode off down the drive, whistling with happiness, certain all would work out somehow.

He retired for the night with the same sort of optimism and woke with it warming him against the coldest morning he ever remembered, with high winds blasting sheets of ice against the windows.

It was the kind of morning that drove everyone to the dining room to be warmed by a blazing fire and drink hot coffee. None wanted to leave the cozy room to so much as retrieve a book from the library. They indulged in idle chitchat about what they would do for Christmas, and who would brave the chill in the hall to fetch them a game or something to read, as no one wanted to force the servants away from the warmth of the kitchen.

"I will go." Tristram rose and stepped into the foyer. Frigid drafts swirled around him. On his way across the marble tiles to the library, he passed a refectory table. A pile of mail rested on a silver tray, waiting for one of the Selkirks to collect and sort. Tristram picked it up, thinking he would carry it to Pierce, and noted his name on a small parcel that had come by courier.

Reading the handwriting on the paper, he thought the draft had found its way to his heart, chilling it. With clumsy fingers, he tore off the plain wrapping and opened the box within.

One of the New York jewelers he had contacted had borne him fruit by collecting and sending one of the Baston-Ward pieces. A scrawled note at the bottom of the bill said:

Sold to me by a lady of average height and excellent form wearing black and a thick veil. Tried to follow, but she disappeared into a waiting cab.

Tristram crushed the note in his fist, then he dropped the jewel to the floor and stomped on it, hoping it would shatter as had the hair comb the night he met Catherine.

The setting bent, but the jewels remained intact—unlike Tristram's heart.

Chapter 12

Therefore, it is of the utmost importance always to leave directions at the door such as, "Mrs. Jones is not at home," "Miss Jones will be home at five o'clock," "Mrs. Jones will be home at 5:30," or Mrs. Jones "is at home" in the library to intimate friends, but "not at home" in the drawing room to acquaintances. It is a nuisance to be obliged to remember either to turn an "in" and "out" card in the hall, or to ring a bell and say, "I am going out," and again, "I have come in." But whatever plan or arrangement you choose, no one at your front door should be left in doubt and then repulsed. It is not only bad manners, it is bad housekeeping.

Emily Price Post

Tristram trudged up the drive of Lake House and reached the door feeling as though the pearl-and-diamond earrings in his pocket weighed what they were worth in British pounds. He could scarcely raise his hand to press the doorbell.

The supercilious butler opened the portal. To the strains of a cello in the distance, he swept his faded blue gaze up and down, and shook his head. "I am sorry you came out in this weather, my lord. Lady Bisterne is not at home."

"I believe you must be mistaken. She told me last week she would be."

And not being at home was as good as a confession, was it not? He had agonized for three days waiting for this afternoon. Seeing her in church, he nearly shook Georgette off his arm in order to plow through the crowd to Catherine.

"She did not inform me as such."

The butler began to shut the door in his face, and Tristram put his foot on the threshold and leaned his shoulder against the massive oak panel to stop him. "Do, please, take her my card." He extracted one from his pocket and pressed it into the butler's gloved hand. "I can wait inside here." He stepped over the threshold.

The butler could either stand there with the door open, or close it and seek out Catherine.

He chose the latter, stalking off like a thwarted three-year-old. A moment later, the cello ceased, replaced by his low rumble of a voice.

"Of course she's at home." Miss Estelle's voice rose loud and clear. "This subterfuge is completely poor management and such bad form." She arrived in the foyer still carrying her bow. "Lord Tristram, I'm sorry you've been kept standing here in the cold of the corridor. Do come into the library, where you can get some warmth. Catherine's edict to not be disturbed doesn't apply to you." She swept around in an arc and strode off down the hall, her skirt flounces bobbing.

Tristram glanced the butler's way and smiled before following Estelle to the library door.

Estelle didn't deign to knock. She twisted the handle and flung the portal wide. "You are at home to Lord Tristram, are you not?" She gestured for him to precede her into the chamber without giving her sister a chance to answer.

The mere sight of her warmed him inside.

Until she looked up from a sheaf of mail before her and her face went dark. "I said not to be disturbed under any circumstances. The vocalist for Mrs. Henry's charity soiree has come down with some ailment and cannot perform. Now I have three days to find a replacement."

"You need look no further," Estelle said, and left the room, closing the door behind her.

Catherine sighed and fixed her gaze on Tristram. "Mama takes a day to rest and the household staff forgets its direction. In other words, why were you let in?"

"Your butler had no choice." He closed the distance between them and stood gazing down at her, his heart aching. "Catherine, you cannot avoid me."

She rose. "I must. I will not hurt Georgette again."

"If Georgette cannot work out for herself that I have no interest in her, she is deluding herself. But my call today has to do with this, not us." He drew the box from his pocket, flipped off the lid and set it on the desk between them.

She glanced down at the earrings, and her face paled. "Where did they come from?"

"A jeweler in New York, two days after you were in the city."

Something like a groan escaped her lips, and she closed her eyes. "And you think I am so foolish I would sell them this close to home knowing you are looking for them?"

"No, I don't. It's too much of a coincidence, but you're the only person who can help me learn the truth."

Her eyes widened. "You believe I'm innocent at last?"

"Yes." He hesitated, then held out his hand. "You will help me."

"I told you everything I know. Except—" She drew one of the earrings from the box and rubbed one of the pearls against a tooth, then held the bauble in front of her, brows knit. "The pearls are real enough."

"How do you know?"

"If you scrape one against your teeth, a real pearl will feel gritty. But the diamonds... The light is too poor today to see inclusions or those little light refractions that distinguish real diamonds. I never would have questioned it except for those…combs." Her voice faltered on the word, the reminder of her husband's false wedding gift.

Tristram rounded the desk to stand beside her—he could not stand to see the pain in her eyes when she spoke of her husband. He needed to be near her, inhaling her spring flower scent, and he wanted to lend her comfort with his nearness. "Surely a jeweler would inspect the jewels before buying the piece."

"Still, they might have inspected the pearls and not gone further when they learned they were real. Pearls, after all, are difficult to falsify. And not all jewelers and pawnbrokers are good at their craft."

"Or they count on the buyer to be ignorant enough to accept the false for true."

"And charge the buyer as though they were real?" She shook her head. "I'd rather not think people are that untrustworthy, but if I could be an untrustworthy friend, I don't see why someone couldn't be an untrustworthy businessman."

"Catherine." He brushed his thumb along her cheek to turn her face toward him. "Georgette holds nothing against you. What is done is done. You won't do it again."

"Does Georgette believe I won't hurt her again?"

"She should."

But Catherine would give him up for Georgette's sake. He wanted to pound his fist against something until his frustration burned itself out.

Chest tight, he turned his attention to the task at hand. "I suppose there's one way to find out if this is a real diamond. Do you have a penknife?"

She handed him the earring and drew out the center drawer of the desk. A moment later, she located the sort of small knife, its hilt shiny from the patina of age and inlaid with mother-of-pearl. It looked old enough to have been in the family for a hundred years, but the blade was honed to razor sharpness. Tristram applied the point to the edge of the setting and popped one of the diamonds into his palm. Then he glanced up. "Do you have a bit of glass you don't care if you ruin?"

She went to the mantel and took down a framed photograph of two ladies too-wrapped in mufflers to identify.

"This should do." She gave him the picture. "An impromptu race with skating chairs when I was seventeen. Georgette and I won."

"A skating chair?"

"Once the lake freezes solid, we'll have skating parties and I'll show you what a skating chair is."

"When does that happen?"

"Near Christmas."

It hurt him to think that he might not be here to see Catherine demonstrate a skating chair, or do anything else, for that matter.

He turned his attention to the diamond. "I could damage it. The picture, that is, not the diamond—if it is a diamond."

She shrugged. "This is more important than a picture of youthful silliness. You can't even see our faces."

"But your parents know it's you."

"They'll understand—if they ever have to know." She took the photograph from him and laid it on the desk. "Go ahead."

Cringing at the idea of marring a picture of Catherine, he picked up the diamond and ran one of the faceted edges along the glass plate. Nothing happened beyond the merest hint of a scratch. He pressed harder. Still nothing.

He looked at Catherine and shook his head. "It's false."

"I see that." Her eyes were wet. "Did I cause all this trouble for false coin?"

"All this trouble?" Tristram's hand flattened on the desk, the artificial diamond tumbling from his fingers to skitter across the surface. "What do you mean by that?"

Surely she wasn't going to confess she had taken the jewels after all. As much as he wanted to cable home just to prove his father wrong, he did not want Catherine to be the culprit.

She dabbed at her eyes with one of those black-bordered handkerchiefs that he hated to see her use. "I thought Edwin might have held me in some regard if he was willing to marry me, but I learned that wasn't true. I thought having a title would make me important, but it didn't. It's all false coin, like the jewels. The real ones have vanished like my belief that I could have anything I wanted proved false." A sob escaped her and fresh tears dampened her handkerchief. "Now I don't know what to believe in."

His heart breaking for her pain, Tristram wrapped his arms around her and cradled her head against his shoulder. "Not everything is false. Jesus's love for us isn't. That's the most important thing to remember, even if perhaps it's most difficult to do so when those on earth who should love us, fail."

"I know. I know. And my family loves me. Or so I like to think. But perhaps they put up with me because they want to make a show of their faithfulness in front of my detractors for the sake of family pride. Perhaps God only tolerates me because He made promises." She clung to his shoulders, quiet and still in his arms. If she still wept, she did so in silence.

The feel of her in his arms needing his comfort felt so much like love, he was overwhelmed.

No, he chastised himself, he couldn't love her until he trusted her completely. But oh, how her nearness made his heart sing.

He touched her smoothly upswept hair. If only—

The library door burst open. "Catherine, Lord Tristram, do come join the rest and listen to my new composition. We can— Oh." Estelle's voice broke off.

Catherine jerked back. Her face paled, and the hand gripping the handkerchief flew to her lips as though she were about to be sick.

Tristram turned more slowly to face a veritable throng in the doorway—Estelle, Florian, Pierce, Ambrose…and Georgette.

Catherine had a strange moment of reflection as she stood there and time seemed to come to a halt. She realized she was rather good at organizing everyone's life but her own. In the month since she'd returned to Tuxedo Park, she had planned three charity events, taken over much of the household management from Mama and ensured Estelle attended at least half of the social events to which she was invited. The busier she was, the less she thought about how Edwin had hurt her, how Tristram still half believed she was guilty…and of Tristram himself—the kiss, the snowball fight, the way the mere sight of him could melt her.

But for all her ability to keep a half dozen juggler's balls in the air without hitting the floor, she could not control her love for Tristram, her wish to cling to his strength or her urge to cling to him even when she'd heard others coming.

Her head had told her to let go. Her heart had said to hang on. And there stood Georgette, staring at her as though she'd kicked a puppy.

She made herself laugh as though she were tossing off something unimportant. "I am overtired from all these events I'm planning. Imagine me crying over something as nonsensical as a broken earring." She scooped up the bauble denuded of one of its false diamonds and dropped it into the box. "I expect a jeweler can repair it. Lord Tristram, why don't you go hear the performance. I have two days until this tea party and some of the details are not yet set. Georgette, will you stay and help me?"

"I think I'd like that." Georgette took a tentative step through the doorway.

"You don't want to go home, Georgie?" Pierce asked.

"No, I'll stay." She moved more quickly to the desk.

Tristram moved in the opposite direction, heading toward the others. "I'd like to go back with you, Pierce."

"Stay and listen to one piece," Estelle urged. "I call this one 'Joy.'"

The men departed with Estelle. Catherine swept the earrings into a desk drawer and drew the lists for the tea to the center of the desk.

"Wait." Georgette leaned forward and picked up the artificial diamond. "You don't want to lose this."

Oh, but she wished she could.

"I suppose not." Catherine placed the cut crystal in with the earrings. When she looked up, Georgette was gazing at the picture.

"We had so much fun together as girls, didn't we? When did we start finding our social prestige was more important than our friendship?"

Catherine sank onto her chair. She should offer coffee or tea, but didn't possess the energy to rise and ring the bell. "Perhaps when we started listening to others tell us what was expected of us."

"Marry well. If not money, then rank and family." Georgette perched on another chair, still holding the picture. "We don't have money like some have, but my mother's side has family back to the *Mayflower*. But you VanDorns have the income and the name. It's always eaten up my mother and grandmother with envy. They were convinced you would steal everything from me."

"And I did." Catherine reached across the desk, though couldn't reach Georgette. "I won't do it again, Georgette. Lord Tristram is a kind-hearted man, and he was giving me comfort. That is all."

Georgette pursed her lips and flicked her gaze to a point above Catherine's head, then inclined her head. "Of course." She sounded anything but convinced.

"Georgie—"

"Now," Georgette hastened to speak over Catherine, "you need my assistance with something for the tea?"

Understanding that the subject of Tristram was closed between her and Georgette, Catherine turned the conversation fully to the charity event. "I have no idea which is the best way to set up the ballroom." Catherine prattled on about table placement, the sort of beverages that would be served, the finger sandwiches and cookies and cakes. Then they moved on to a discussion of the first skating party of the year. They did not mention Tristram again or answer the question surely at the top of Georgette's mind—why was Tristram alone with Catherine to begin with?

When Georgette had departed, Catherine realized yet one more difficulty. If Georgette did convince Tristram to wed him, she was likely to learn about the jewelry and his lingering suspicions that Catherine lay behind the theft. And what would happen between their families then?

For the next two days, Catherine kept herself so busy with preparations for the charity tea that she had no time to think about the possibility of Tristram and Georgette marrying, and was too weary at night not to sleep.

The morning of the tea dawned bright and clear. Catherine took the automobile to the clubhouse to look into the decorations, ensuring that the flowers had arrived on the morning train. She supervised their placement and, at last satisfied with the arrangements, she went home to dress.

For the second time since returning home, she donned one of her gowns from Paris. It was white lace with a wide neckline, filled in from the shoulders to a high neck with sheer lace. She wore pearl eardrops, and pearl combs in her hair beneath a wide-brimmed hat of white straw trimmed with white roses. White wouldn't raise as many eyebrows as had the mauve, and it still wasn't first mourning. She wished she could tell the critics that mourning a man who barely acknowledged her existence was hypocritical of her. They would likely tell her that she had made the choice to marry him and her husband deserved her respect.

She cringed at the thought. She hadn't respected Edwin. Once she knew he intended to behave as though he had no wife, she used the power of her money over him.

And now here she was, using the power that his title gave her over much of the Tuxedo Club's female population. After all, why else would the older Selkirk ladies buy tickets to this particular tea for the first time in five years? Their arrival brought a hush over the room—a hush followed by excited chatter. Catherine served the Selkirk ladies herself, aided by Georgette and Mrs. Daisy Baker, another friend from Mrs. Graham's academy. They dispensed tea and hot chocolate and directed the guests to the tiered plates of cakes and sweets.

Catherine poured, sent for fresh tea and poured some more. Her arm grew weary, but her heart sang at how smoothly everything was going. She poured one more cup, then glanced up to hand it to the next person in line and looked straight into Tristram's jade-green eyes.

He managed to take the cup and bow without releasing her gaze. "May I call tomorrow, my lady? I'd like to retrieve those earrings."

Catherine flashed a glance at Georgette, busy serving Ambrose and Florian.

"Tomorrow," he said, and left before she could protest.

The majority of the ticket holders having arrived, Catherine abandoned the tea-serving table and began to circulate through the room. On the stage, Estelle, Ambrose and Florian began to play Christmas carols.

Most of the ladies and handful of gentlemen present

greeted Catherine with cordiality, with only a few back-handed compliments slipped in.

"Lovely dress. You look more like a bride than a widow."

"Hanging out for another title?"

Catherine ignored the remarks and continued the hostess duties Mama had performed for the past ten years. Her mother presided over a table chatting and laughing with her friends, pretty and content.

Catherine paused beside her and kissed her cheek. "Are you happy with everything?"

"How can I not be when I have two such admirable daughters?"

Tristram sat at the next table with one other gentleman and three young ladies. Three more empty chairs suggested Estelle, Ambrose and Florian had taken their refreshments there before going onto the stage.

Tristram and the other man rose at Catherine's approach. She didn't recognize him or the young ladies.

"Lady Bisterne," Tristram said, "allow me to introduce the Beaumonts. They bought the property next to the Selkirks last year."

They all made proper "how do you do" responses, then the Beaumonts returned to their chairs. Tristram remained standing.

She motioned for one of the waiters to come clear away their plates. "I hope you are enjoying yourself." She glanced at Tristram's cup. "Hot chocolate? I thought I poured you tea."

"You did. It was not to my taste and I was feeling rather chilled."

"But I ensured the tea was perfect. I don't know why—" She narrowed her eyes. "Are you all right? You've gone quite pale."

He was not only pale, a sheen of perspiration had broken out on his face, and he gripped the back of his chair. "I think I should get some fresh air."

His companions at the table had ceased their conversation and were staring.

Catherine stepped forward to offer him her arm, but when he released the chair, he swayed, took a staggering step forward and collapsed onto the ballroom floor.

Chapter 13

Should a guest be taken ill, she must assure him that he is not giving the slightest trouble; at the same time nothing that can be done for his comfort must be overlooked.

Emily Price Post

Catherine rushed to catch Tristram, but Mr. Beaumont reached him first, lowering him to the floor. Around her, ladies gasped in horror.

"Should I send someone to fetch the doctor, my lady?"

"Find a place to carry him first." Catherine kept her voice calm. To those who had seen the incident, she offered them an assuring smile and a waved hand. "He's a wounded war hero."

She said the words as though that explained why he would collapse in the middle of a charity tea, while the music continued in joyous celebration upon the stage.

Catherine returned her attention to Tristram, so pale, and she wasn't entirely sure he still breathed. She wasn't entirely sure *she* still breathed. Her breath felt trapped in her lungs, about to burst with a wail.

Please, Lord. Please let him be all right.

Tristram didn't drink spirits. He couldn't be inebriated. Had his concussion of a few weeks ago caused some sort of relapse? Or was he ill for other reasons, something contagious, perhaps?

No matter, she would catch the plague and she wouldn't care. She must see to his welfare.

"I live across the way in the bachelor's quarters," Mr. Beaumont was saying. "I'm happy to carry him to my room."

"Thank you."

She knew that she couldn't see him there, but she could not concern herself with that now. Tristram needed warmth, comfort and care.

"Yes, carry him there. Thank you." As though nothing were truly wrong, she continued her circuit of the room, ending up back at the serving table, where Georgette seized her arm.

"What happened?"

"Tristram has collapsed. Dr. Rushmore is on his way. Right now he's being taken to the bachelor house."

Georgette's golden brows drew together. "I do hope this doesn't mean there's weak blood in his family. One does hear things of English aristocrats, and I don't want to pass that sort of thing to my children."

"Your…children?" Catherine stared at her old friend. "Has he made you an offer?"

"No, but I am determined to marry him. We get on well, and he'll take me away from this confining life."

No declarations like "I love him and intend to win him." She was simply *determined* to wed him.

If Tristram were all right—and Catherine prayed that he was—he deserved better than to be snared by someone chasing after his title. That was no different than a poor man going after a lady's dowry.

She had been there, pursuing Edwin for his title so she could have the highest rank of any of her friends, yet she reviled Edwin for exploiting her money for his own gain.

She claimed she wished Edwin had cared for her, yet what had she done to care for him? She showed him as little respect in death as she had in life, shunning her mourning far too soon, flaunting her disdain for him with her mauve dress just over a year after his death.

Turning away from Georgette with the excuse of inspecting the contents of the tea and chocolate pots, she voiced a silent prayer. *Lord, I cannot ask Edwin for forgiveness, but I can ask You. Please forgive my selfishness, my greed, my lack of remembering that You are what is important.*

She said a prayer that Tristram would be all right. She wanted to pray that the Lord would show Georgette that she was making a terrible mistake if she didn't love Tristram, but she would not even think to put that much of a wedge between her friend and what she wanted. She couldn't, even if it was for Georgette's and Tristram's well-being. A reunion of families was already taking place before her eyes, as Mama sat down to tea and talked with the older Selkirk ladies. That peace, that ending of the gossip and nasty remarks, was too precious to risk.

Head whirling, she felt like Tristram had looked in those last moments before he fell—pale and shaken. She touched her handkerchief to her brow.

"Are you taken ill, as well?" Georgette whispered in her ear. "I surely hope nothing was wrong with any of the food."

"I haven't partaken of any of the food."

But Tristram had. He said the tea was not to his taste, yet Ambrose's and Florian's cups had sat empty upon the table and they had drunk the same tea. Nothing had happened to them. They were just now finishing up a melody and taking their bows to much applause.

His mostly full cup of tea had been pushed toward the arrangement of poinsettias and greenery in the center of the table, and replaced by hot chocolate acquired just after she left the beverage table.

Not to his taste, he'd said about the tea, as though it tasted odd. Too sweet? Too bitter? He took just a bit of milk in his tea.

Her stomach seized up at the notion in her mind. Yet it wasn't out of the question. Someone, after all, had sent him to Lake House, had smashed him on the head and left him in the snow. Hitting was more likely a thing a man would do.

Poison, however, was considered a lady's trick.

The blow had taken place outside her house, the illness at her charity tea. Two incidents that could easily be blamed on her.

"Excuse me." Spinning on her heel, she forced herself to move at a sedate pace, though what she truly wanted to do was run—run to Tristram, ensure his well-being, talk to him about what she feared.

Not until she reached the doorway did she realize she should have attempted to retrieve Tristram's teacup. But no, she had motioned for a waiter to clear the table, an action that could be taken as her trying to destroy evidence.

Her heart commenced racing like a polo pony. She pressed a hand to her chest and breathed deeply. It worked for a few moments until Dr. Rushmore strode through the doorway.

"Doctor?" She nearly pounced upon the poor man.

He touched her cheek. "You're pale, my lady. Are you ill, as well?"

"Only anxious."

"He will be fine in a day or two of rest. Something he ate disagreed with him."

"Do you think something could be wrong with the food?" she asked. "Will others be ill?"

Dr. Rushmore smiled. "I don't think so. Sometimes people can't tolerate certain foods. We don't know why yet, but we're working on finding out." He patted her arm as though he were old enough to be her father, which was decades from the truth. "I expect your beau will call as soon as he's well."

"He's not my—"

Several ladies emerged from the ballroom to surround the doctor, inviting him to come in for a hot drink and sandwiches. No one expected the doctor, making a pittance in comparison with the income of the Tuxedo Park residents, to pay for a ticket.

Like an automaton, Catherine returned to her duties. Guests were beginning to leave, drifting out in twos and threes. She thanked as many as she could for coming. She supervised the waiters in cleaning up the tables and made arrangements for the flowers to go to the church and the leftover food to the needy.

All had gone well except for Tristram's mysterious and sudden illness.

At last, she was able to go home, where she could sit without distraction and run through the details surrounding Tristram. He hadn't liked the tea. Some people couldn't tolerate certain foods, but Tristram could tolerate tea in great quantities. Nothing was wrong with the tea. No one else had gotten ill. Perhaps something in the sandwiches or cakes had caused his collapse, but instinct told her no. That tea not being to his taste haunted her.

"Because some people can't tolerate poison." There, she had said it aloud—given voice to her fears.

But who and why? To make her look bad? That would make her look guilty—an attempt on Tristram's life. The real jewel thief would perhaps rid himself of his pursuer and turn everyone's attention to Catherine.

But who? No one at the serving tables. They lacked opportunity to steal the jewels. Indeed, Florian was the only person who had been inside Bisterne since Edwin's death—other than Catherine. Ambrose was Edwin's friend, but he hadn't paid a call at Bisterne for months before her husband died. Someone else passing by? Strangers about whom Catherine knew nothing?

Her mind spinning around and around the same notions, Catherine buried herself in details for the next charity event to distract her thoughts, and tried not to think about Tristram. She could do nothing more than send a note around to Mr. Beaumont and request information as to Tristram's welfare. She received no response from Mr. Beaumont, nor did she hear from Florian and Ambrose.

But Tristram himself called on her the following morning.

Conscious of how easily he could have died at the tea, Tristram was anxious to speak to Catherine, to learn what she thought of the incident. She was easily the one to suspect. Too easily. Yet who else would want to get rid of him?

Catherine received him in the conservatory, where sunlight shimmered off a row of icicles as though she resided in some kind of ice palace. The white snow and colorless ice emphasized the deep blue of her gown and the sunlight brought out the red highlights in her hair. The sight of her robbed him of breath, of even a whisper that she could try to harm anyone, especially him.

"Are you going to come in or stand there and stare?" The corners of her lips twitched up.

He strode into the room to meet her in front of the windows where he had kissed her in a moment of madness he would like to repeat. "I was appreciating the scenery—and you." He shoved his hands into his pockets to keep himself from touching her. "Are you well?"

"I'm quite well. It's you who concerns me." She touched his arm as she gazed up at him. "Are you doing all right?

Does the doctor know you're up and about? May I send for tea?"

"I think I'm off tea for a while, but I would like some of that hot cider, if you have any."

"We always do, at least through Christmas." She sent for the hot drink, then seated herself on a sofa to give him leave to be seated.

He took a chair adjacent to her so he could better look at her.

She met his gaze without flinching. "Lord Tristram, I believe you were poisoned?"

"We don't beat around any bushes, do we?" That was as much levity as he could manage. "Why do you ask something so…serious?"

"Rarely does an illness come on so quickly, and you said the tea wasn't to your taste, but I made certain that tea was perfect. I put nothing in it but a little milk, so it should have been to your taste."

"Yet somehow, someone managed to insert a rather hefty dose of potassium bromide."

She jerked upright. "How do you know? The waiters cleared the table."

"Not fast enough. I regained consciousness soon enough to tell Beaumont to gather my cup from the table and give it to the physician."

"So you suspected, too?" She leaned back against the cushions and closed her eyes. "Did you suspect me again?"

"You had the best opportunity."

She opened her eyes wide enough to glare at him.

He leaned forward and covered her hand where it rested on the arm of the sofa. "Too good an opportunity. Like that last pair of earrings, it's too coincidental, too much like someone wanting me to think it's you trying to hurt me or get rid of stolen jewels."

"Hurt you?" She turned over her hand and laced her fingers with his. "Tristram, can potassium bromide not kill?"

"In large enough doses. Fortunately, that large a dose tastes so bitter, no one in his right mind would drink it."

"So whoever put it in your tea is an amateur—" She squeezed his fingers hard enough to hurt. "Let us stop dancing around this topic. Someone might have wanted to kill you. First the blow to your head, and now this."

"I have a feeling if you hadn't come along, someone else would have rescued me from the snow before it was too late. And yesterday, I drank enough to lose consciousness for a few minutes, but not enough to kill me."

"So what's the purpose?"

"To scare me off from here? From pursuing the jewel thief?" He rubbed his thumb over the back of her hand. "To cast more aspersions on you?"

"Or all of those choices."

"Or all of those choices."

"Who is behind all this?"

The arrival of the hot cider, rich with the scent of cinnamon sticks and nutmeg, saved him from having to hedge. He could tell her what he should have known all along, but he wouldn't again question anyone's honesty as he had Catherine's, until he gathered enough evidence.

"Tell me, Catherine, what happened in those last days of Bisterne's life?"

She shook her head. "Nothing unusual. He came home for more money, as he did every quarter. He did some riding and shooting with neighbors, then he went to the safe, took out the jewels and rumbled about how it was such a waste he couldn't sell them so he wouldn't have to live off the largesse of an American female."

"But why couldn't he sell the jewels? They go with the estate, but they're not entailed like property."

"I don't know. I thought some English law prevented him

from doing so. Other than the combs and wedding and engagement rings he gave me, I never wore the jewels. And the combs—" She stopped, and her eyes widened. "He knew they were false. That's why he couldn't sell them."

Tristram inclined his head. "I think you're right. He knew all along someone had traded most of the real stones for false ones, but he might not have been sure which were which, so he dared not risk anyone learning they were artificial if he chose the wrong ones."

"Someone else from the family. It had to be someone else from the family who knew the combination to the safe. His father, perhaps?"

"Or his uncle?"

"Florian's brother?"

She did not suggest Florian himself, but she must be wondering as much as Tristram was if Florian could be behind the attacks and the theft. It would explain his confidence that Estelle and her father would find him acceptable; he knew he possessed money hidden away somewhere.

"Was Ambrose ever at Bisterne?" he asked.

She shook her head. "He despises the country. We met in town once or twice when I managed to get up there for some shopping. Why do you ask? He's not part of the family, is he?"

"No, he's a Wolfe with no Baston-Ward connections. But I'm seeking all avenues."

Her face lit, her sparkling dark eyes upon him. "Does that mean I am no longer guilty?"

"It does. Now I just want to call on you because I quite want to be around you." He drew her hand to his lips. "May I?"

She drew her hand free. "Georgette."

"I keep trying to talk to her about it, but she stops me every time, as though if I don't say it, it won't be true."

"But it could make trouble if she's humiliated again."

"If she is, then it's of her making, not yours."

She released his hand and rose to pace the room. "I'd like you to call on me. But I'm not ready to marry another English heir, especially one Georgette has set her heart upon."

"Is it her heart or her pride?"

She stopped and pressed her fingertips to her temples. "I'm afraid the latter. But can I hurt her pride again and cause another rift amongst the older ladies, among my mother's friends?"

"Are you responsible for their behavior?" Tristram stood and fixed her with a scowl, his body tense with frustration.

She glared back. "Are you responsible for finding the jewels because your father can't be proud of the man you are without you performing some feat?"

"A great deal of money depends on me succeeding."

"Which is something else. How dare he hurt others just to make you prove something that's really none of your concern. This should be managed by proper investigators. Why aren't they on to the jewel thief?"

"To keep it out of public notice."

"Well, if you don't succeed, the public will notice eventually."

"I have to succeed, Catherine. This has gone well beyond me finding a jewel thief. This pursuit could cost me my life."

"You are right in that." Her lower lip quivered. "But I cannot allow you to pay me particular attention, unless Georgette realizes what she's doing."

"And I won't force my presence upon you." He gazed at her, his eyes burning, his heart aching, knowing he loved her to distraction. "I must leave here in three weeks to get home by my father's deadline." He bowed.

"I am going back to the Selkirks to talk to Georgette about my feelings—my lack of feelings—toward her. This cannot continue if I may have a future with you." He gazed at her, his heart about to burst as he awaited a response from Catherine.

She gave him her calm, cool look. "We'll talk about the future when the present is settled."

Frustrated, amused, he held her gaze. "Then I have great motivation to succeed."

As though she sensed his greater determination, Georgette avoided him as much as possible. Indeed, she arranged for him to be out of the house—urging Pierce to take Tristram shooting or ice fishing with the men. Why anyone would voluntarily freeze for fish one could well afford to purchase, Tristram didn't know, but Pierce and his cronies seemed to consider it a feat of manly virtue to withstand the cold for what amounted to only enough fish for hors d'oeuvres at a small gathering had they even kept them.

Tristram rather enjoyed these outdoor activities with other gentlemen. He felt safe from the threatening behavior of others in their company. At the same time, he longed to be with Catherine and ached for just half an hour alone with Georgette. He must seize an opportunity, whether she wished for it or not, and speak with Georgette before he returned to England three days before Christmas.

He thought his opportunity arrived one morning in mid December. Snow had fallen the previous day and most of the night, but the day broke with brilliant sunlight. Ambrose and Florian were discussing calling on Estelle to practice one of her new compositions when Georgette walked into the parlor.

She wore a pink wool suit and creamy lace. She met his gaze and smiled, her eyes soft and warm. "You don't want to hear one of Estelle's compositions, do you, Tristram? It's such a pretty day, I thought we could try the toboggan run at the racket club."

"I can think of few things I'd like more." Beyond seeing Catherine, holding her hands in his, touching her porcelain cheek...

Florian cast him a sympathetic glance, then turned to Georgette. "Come listen to Estelle's composition, and then we'll all go over to the racket club. The ice is thick enough for skating."

"If you like, I'll go." Tristram didn't want to seem too eager.

For nearly two weeks, he had honored Catherine's wishes and hadn't called on her. His heart had to be satisfied with brief greetings at social gatherings they both attended, though she didn't seem to attend many. Much of the past two weeks, Catherine was in the city working on charitable events and shopping with her mother and sister, Tristram learned from Florian, who moped around without Estelle near.

Tristram envied the younger man. If he were free he could walk away from his father's edict and offer for Catherine. Of course, that might be considered too much of the easy road to solving his difficulties with his father.

Riding in the Selkirks' automobile along the well-groomed street leading past houses that offered nothing less than ultimate comfort, Tristram realized that he had lived his life like that road. He took the path into the army because it was easier than fighting with his father about another course of action. He disobeyed orders because that was easier than trying to convince his superiors what they were doing hurt England's cause in the end. Then he accepted his father's ultimatum because it was easier than staying home. Believing Catherine was the jewel thief was easier than trying to find the real culprit. Now staying away from Catherine was easier than forcing a confrontation with Georgette.

How can I call myself a man of God willing to serve Him if I am unwilling to take risks He might demand of me?

He turned to Pierce, who was driving. "Let me out. I want to walk."

"We'll be there in two minutes." Pierce pointed out the obvious, but pulled on the brake.

"And I'll see you in ten."

"But, Tristram," Georgette called from the rumble seat, "walking through this snow is so difficult."

"I know." Tristram waved and set off.

Belching and chugging, the auto pulled away, Georgette waving.

"What would You have me do, Lord?" He asked the question aloud.

No specific answer came to him. When he arrived at Lake House, his trousers sodden, the VanDorns' butler greeted him with considerably more courtesy than the previous visit, and led him straight to the drawing room fire. And there sat Catherine dispensing hot chocolate. She glanced up, saw him approaching her and dropped a china cup onto the hearth. It shattered into a hundred pieces, and Tristram's heart sang.

"I didn't know you were coming." She stooped to gather up the broken china.

"I almost didn't." He bent to help her. "But they mentioned skating, and you promised to show me what a skating chair is."

"I did, didn't I?" Her gaze flicked to the music room, where she could see Georgette through the doorway trying her hand at Estelle's banjo. "Georgette…?"

"No, I've not spoken to her yet. I—" He looked into Catherine's eyes. "I'm a coward. All my life—"

"Tristram." Georgette's voice rang out from the music room doorway. "I'm happy to see you arrived safely. Are you ready to push me in a skating chair?"

"I think that sounds—" He stopped himself. "I'm afraid—" From the corner of his eye, he caught Catherine's quick shake of her head. "Catherine already promised to show me how the skating chairs work."

"I see." Georgette's eyes went as wintry cold as the December sky. "Well, I think it inappropriate for such a recent widow to do something as frivolous as skate."

Tristram's heart sank. She wasn't going to be understanding about his feelings for Catherine. The genteel feuding between the families would start again unless he figured out what to do.

"She's right." Catherine rose, her hands full of china shards. "I should stay here and help Mama with Christmas—"

Tristram turned to her. "Is breaking promises easier than keeping them?"

"That depends on to whom one makes the promise." She glanced toward Georgette, who was watching them closely.

Breaking promises was rarely easier than keeping them. He had made a promise to her. He had made one to his father. Most of all, he had made a promise to his heavenly Father to serve him. But he didn't want to serve the Lord alone. He wanted Catherine at his side, the stubborn, loyal love.

"Does your sister not need a chaperone?" he asked Catherine.

"I do." Estelle tucked one hand beneath Georgette's elbow. "As is, we have too many gentlemen."

Georgette looked away from Tristram and Catherine, and gave Estelle a smile. "Of course. How silly of me. We'll find more for our party, if they're not already there."

One phone call by Estelle ensured that the racket club teemed with young people by the time the Selkirk and Van-Dorn parties arrived. Ladies and gentlemen alike donned black skates and headed to the lake. Someone found Tristram a pair that fit and he donned them with considerable doubt.

"I haven't been on ice since I was a schoolboy. We don't get weather cold enough to freeze water thick enough most of the time."

"But all I remember is freezing cold weather." Catherine shivered. "Living in Bisterne was like having an icehouse for a home."

"And not something you wish to repeat?" Georgette bent to strap on her own skates. "Last one on the ice is a rotten egg." She headed toward the ice.

"No takers, Georgie. We can't compete with you." Catherine glanced at Tristram without looking at him directly. "She has always been the fastest. That's why we let her push the skating chairs instead of riding in one like the rest of us ladies do."

"And where are these famed chairs?"

"On the lake." Georgette set out across the snowy ground, as though walking in skates were as easy as walking in flat shoes. Catherine followed not as fast, but just as gracefully as Georgette. Tristram moved more slowly, testing his balance on the skates. He hadn't been on blades for at least twelve years, and the iron runners didn't afford much support to someone unaccustomed to the sport, especially with the distraction of Catherine ahead of him. He wouldn't even think about how he'd fare on slippery ice.

Georgette reached the edge of the lake, stepped onto the frozen surface and glided off like a swan, turning slowly, then spinning and leaping, creating a ballet on ice.

"She's beautiful," Catherine said.

"She is lovely." Tristram rested his gloved hand on Catherine's shoulder. "But she is rather a schemer, which somewhat diminishes her attractions."

"Whatever do you mean?"

"She won't give me an opportunity to talk to her alone."

"She knows you won't marry her. I saw it in her eyes back at Lake House." Catherine looked up at him through tears sparkling on her lashes. "I've solved nothing in coming home."

"You've done nothing wrong. I was pursuing you, not the other way around."

"But—"

He touched one finger to her lips. "Now, where are the chairs you were going to show me?" He glanced around and saw two objects that resembled dining room chairs with arms and, on the bottom, runners attached from front legs to back on either side.

Florian, Estelle and Ambrose joined them.

"What do you do with a contraption like that?" Ambrose asked.

"We make teams and have races." Catherine bit her lip. "Perhaps you should go to Georgette's team, Tristram. It looks like groups are forming."

Tristram glanced toward where Georgette was forming two lines a few yards away at the edge of the ice, then shook his head. "I'm staying on whatever team you choose." He headed for the chairs.

"I'm going to Georgie's team," Estelle said over her shoulder. "I want to win, and Georgette's teams always win."

"So do I." Florian sailed off after her.

"I think those two are up to something," Ambrose said.

Catherine shrugged. "As long as they are here in our sight, it can't be too bad. Will you partner me, Ambrose?"

"No, thank you." He scanned the line and headed for a pretty girl Tristram had often seen Catherine's brother, Paul, wooing.

No matter, Ambrose wouldn't get any further with her than he had with the heiress in New York. "You've been thwarted in your attempt to keep me away." Tristram tucked his hand beneath Catherine's elbow. "And Florian and Estelle have evened the numbers on the other team."

"You should trade with Florian for the sake of peace."

"Too late."

Indeed, the game was on. The first two pairs arranged themselves at the edge of a marker made with someone's muffler. One of the men counted down to go, and the skaters shot out across the ice. They looked rather absurd with the lady's skirts flowing back along the legs of the chair, even the chair itself sailing across the ice like a bath chair on a boardwalk. Most of the observers leaped up and down cheering on their teammates. They laughed when one couple in the second run got skates, chair legs and a torn flounce on the lady's gown tangled and the two of them ended up sitting in the chair together. Whoops and hollers and cries to hurry rang through the crystal, bright air. The other team became a full length ahead. Ambrose, surprisingly swift, helped make up some of the slack with his lightweight companion, also graceful and swift on her skates.

And then Tristram and Catherine's turn came.

Catherine settled into the chair and Tristram took his place behind, glad of the chair's support. He glanced at Georgette. Poised on her toes in the event her team needed her to go again, she frowned in his and Catherine's direction, clearly displeased by their pairing. He smiled and returned his attention to Catherine. "Ready?"

"I'm ready." She gripped the arms. "It's the return journey that worries me. I haven't skated in five years."

"It's been longer for me."

But they were off, too slow at first to please their teammates, then gathering speed as he gained some confidence. They moved faster and faster, the cries of their team roaring behind them. Only a yard or two behind the other team, they reached the second muffler line marker. Catherine tried to stand. Her right foot shot out ahead of her. She grabbed the chair arm for support. With the rasp of steel on ice, the chair shot backward, knocking Tristram to the ice on one side and tossing Catherine to her knees on the other.

For a moment, neither of them made a sound, while their team shouted and groaned on the shore. Then Tristram grabbed the push bar for balance. Upright, he released the chair to go to Catherine's aid, and the chair soared across the ice, executed a pirouette and came to a standstill a dozen yards away.

"The chair is a better skater than either of us." Tristram reached down to take Catherine's hands.

She laughed up at him as she struggled to get her feet beneath her. "We had better catch up with it."

"Then allow me." He tucked his hands beneath her elbows and lifted.

With the sun beating down, the surface had grown more slick. Both sets of blades took on minds of their own and Tristram ended up on his knees holding Catherine far too close.

Or just close enough—close enough that the merest lowering of his head would bring his lips in contact with hers. He didn't give himself time to think whether or not he should; he lowered his head that fraction and kissed her because he couldn't stop himself any more than iron filings could stop themselves from sticking to a magnet. And once his lips contacted hers, he didn't care who saw them.

From far away came a smattering of applause, a few hoots and one cry of protest. For far too few moments, Tristram held Catherine to him, her lips warm beneath his. Then cold from the wet ice seeped through his trousers and he remembered where he was, and the size and makeup of the audience.

He raised his head. Her eyes were still closed, her face bright with sunshine and wonder.

"They're coming to our aid. Or perhaps to string me up."

"Or me, the wicked widow." She half turned to face the rescuers. Ambrose, Pierce and Georgette were sailing across the ice, their faces grim.

"I will not apologize." Tristram took Catherine's hand.

She shook her head, and kept a grip on his fingers. His heart soared like the skaters racing toward them. She hadn't rejected him. She wasn't rejecting him.

Yet she still might, if the faces of the others were indications of trouble.

Catherine reached out for Georgette. "I am so sorry. I never meant—"

"Never mind that." Pierce hauled her to her runners. "A call just came into the clubhouse for you to come home at once."

Chapter 14

The bride gives a "wedding present" or a "wedding ring" or both to the groom, if she especially wants to. (Not necessary, nor even customary.)

Emily Price Post

Reality slammed into Catherine like a streetcar. What was she thinking, kissing Tristram—kissing Tristram in front of everyone, in front of Georgette. She was creating another scandal.

"What urgent message?" Catherine thought to ask as Pierce gripped her hand, pulling her toward the shore like a child's toy on wheels, leaving Tristram behind with Georgette and Ambrose.

"I don't know. A call came into the club saying for you to go home immediately."

A crisis with one of the charity events, no doubt, a frantic hostess on the phone or sending telegrams.

Catherine increased her stride once on shore. "Where's Estelle?"

"I don't know." Pierce glanced around. "I expect she heard of the summons and left already. Get your skates off, I'll drive you."

And keep her away from Tristram.

Catherine complied in the event the call was a true emergency. She proved fumble-fingered and unbalanced in her haste to enter the clubhouse. She looked around for Georgette as she removed her skates. She saw neither the old friend she had once again betrayed, nor Tristram. They had likely walked off alone, Georgette remonstrating or pleading, Tristram explaining—how? What would he say? That "it was a madness of the moment"?

But it wasn't. He loved her. She loved him. It was foolish of her. He was another impoverished English lord, courtesy title or direct heir to marquessate or not. He would likely not find the jewels now unless—

She caught her breath. No, no, not so. He wouldn't woo her with sweet kisses and tender words, figuring he could benefit from her trust fund and still prove she was the thief to please his father. No one was that mercenary.

Yet the past reared its head, Edwin telling her he had loved her all along and her accepting his words as truth because she wanted to believe she was entering a love match and not one that was purely selfish. The past waved a banner of distrust in her face, blinding her with tears.

"I suggest you go into the city for a few days." Pierce delivered his admonition as he drew the auto up to the front steps of Lake House. "You've proven once again you can't be loyal to a friend."

"I know. I'm sorry." She didn't know what else to say.

Pierce rounded the vehicle to help her down, and the butler flung open the front door.

"Lady Bisterne, so glad you're here. Mrs. VanDorn is in her boudoir."

Catherine raced up the steps to Mama's boudoir and opened the door without knocking. "Mama, what's wrong? Did Mrs. Rutledge fail to—"

"No." Mama slumped over her escritoire, a handkerchief pressed to her eyes. "Not that charity ball." She lowered the handkerchief and gazed at Catherine. "It's Estelle. She's eloped."

"But I just saw her." Catherine sank onto the chaise longue. "No more than…"

When had she seen her last? Right before the races started. Thirty minutes? Forty?

"How do you know?" Catherine demanded.

Mama held out a crumpled and damp sheet of paper covered with musical notes on one side and scrawled writing on the other. Catherine took it and read the message in a glance. *Florian and I eloped.*

"Not another one." Catherine dropped her head into her hands. "We can't bear another scandal. Estelle's reputation. Our reputation. Our family honor."

She had done damage to her family five years ago. She swore she wouldn't do it again under any circumstances. Yet she had let Tristram kiss her—she had kissed Tristram— right in front of half the young people in Tuxedo Park.

She squeezed her skull between her palms. "Did you tell Papa or Paul?"

"I won't do it over the telephone. I'll have to wait until they get home unless you go into the city on the next train and tell them in person."

Catherine's head shot up. "It can wait until they reach home. There's nothing we can do from the city."

"You can make discreet enquiries about train passengers from here and in which direction they departed." Mama groaned. "Where have we gone wrong with our girls? It isn't as though we forced you into loveless marriages."

Catherine rested her hand on Mama's shoulder. "You were possibly too indulgent, allowing Estelle to devote herself to her music, though not doing so would have been a shame. She is so very gifted. And as for me… I let the hunger for status amongst the people here rule my heart instead of the faith you taught me." She embraced her mother, then strode to the door. "I'll do what I can to find her."

She caught up a hat and her handbag from her room and

then ran down the steps, calling for the automobile to be brought around.

It already waited for her in the front. Catherine climbed in and they chugged toward the gates and outside the fence to the train station, where another train wasn't due for an hour. An hour to wait, to pace around the waiting area, to fret over Estelle's madcap behavior, over her own terrible behavior with Tristram, over her inability to set the past behind after all.

Lord, why can I not make wise choices?

Seeing the station master, she rushed across the room. He had known her family for years. He had been the last familiar face in Tuxedo Park who had seen her when she eloped. "Sir, can you tell me what train Miss Estelle Van-Dorn took?"

"Miss Estelle?" He scratched his head beneath his railroad cap. "Hmm. I don't believe I've seen her today."

Catherine stepped back. "Then how—?" she began. Then she clamped her mouth shut. "Thank you."

If they hadn't taken a train, how had they departed? They wouldn't have access to an automobile. But Florian could drive a carriage.

She left the station and headed through the village to the livery. Her actions were going to create a stir. They wouldn't be able to keep Estelle's elopement with Florian quiet for long. But that wouldn't matter if Catherine could bring Estelle back. Once she returned, any hint of gossip would die down. People would put the temporary disappearance down to a youthful lark.

When Catherine hastened into the livery, the liveryman was just unharnessing a horse from a buggy, the former looking weary. He shouted something to a stable hand, then approached Catherine, his face puzzled. People from inside the fence rarely rented horses or buggies from him.

"Ma'am?"

"Has a young man rented a horse from you today? Dark hair, green eyes, about this tall?" She held her hand a few inches over her head.

The liveryman nodded at the horse the hand led toward the stable. "He picked him up around two hours ago. Just sent him back lathered like he'd been in a race. And if he takes sick 'cause of it—"

"Send the bill to the VanDorn household. Where did he come back from?"

"The man didn't say. Just left him here and walked off." He narrowed his eyes. "Is there something illegal at foot?"

"I don't think so. Just a guest being foolish." She offered him a winning smile and retraced her steps to the train station.

The man who had returned the carriage for Florian and Estelle would have to get back to wherever he came from somehow. If he didn't have a vehicle, the train was the only way.

The train she intended to take into the city had departed, and a lone passenger slumped on a bench. Catherine approached him, conscious of the station master staring at her from behind the ticket counter. "Did you just deliver a buggy to the livery?"

"Yes, ma'am." The man didn't bother to rise. "Got paid well, too, to keep quiet."

"How well?"

He told her.

She paid him twice as much to talk.

And then she sat to wait for the next train. Outside, dusk fell. Incoming trains began to disgorge passengers returning from the city. She scanned the crowds for Papa and Paul, then thought to duck her head so none of the others who knew her would see she sat waiting for a train alone, a train that arrived at last, delayed by snow upstate. Down the line everything remained clear, giving Florian and Estelle too much of a head start.

Catherine sprang to her feet and headed for the doors, pushing against the inflowing tide of city workers.

"Catherine?" Her name rang out over the general hubbub. "Catherine, wait!"

Catherine spun around on the edge of the platform. Surely her ears deceived her.

They did not. Georgette shoved through the crowd and grasped Catherine's hand. "Thank the Lord I found you. Your mother said you probably left already, but I had to try. I'd have come after you—" She stopped to catch her breath. "You must come."

"Come where?" Catherine blinked in confusion.

"All aboard," the conductor bellowed.

Catherine took a step toward Georgette, then stopped. "I have to get on this train."

"No, you have to come back to my house." Georgette dashed a hand across her eyes. "It's Tristram. He—"

The train's whistle blew, drowning her words.

"Tristram what?" Catherine grasped Georgette's arm.

"He's been badly injured." Georgette's shout cut through the whistle, the hiss of steam from the boiler sounded like the scream rising in Catherine's throat. "He's asking for you."

Catherine pulled at the fingers of her gloves, torn between listening to Georgette and going to Tristram, and going after her sister to prevent the scandal already in the making.

The train would leave in no more than a minute or two. Catherine must be on it or Estelle would be lost somewhere in the city, or even on a ship across the Atlantic.

"I have to be on that train." Her heart squeezed. She teetered as though physically pulled in two directions.

"He could die if his injuries are bad enough." Georgette

grasped Catherine's shoulders and shook her. "If you don't come, then you truly have betrayed our friendship because you don't deserve a man who loves you as he does."

"My sister... The scandal... I—"

"Last chance, ma'am." The conductor called to Catherine across the empty platform.

Perhaps her last chance to see Tristram, her last chance for love. She could lose him forever. Estelle had made her own choice to create a scandal. Mama had made the choice to keep it quiet and not make telephone calls that could have stopped her younger daughter.

If Catherine chose not to go to him to protect her family's reputation, it was the sort of selfish action that had caused so much trouble in the past. If she wanted to truly set the past behind her, she needed to go to Tristram and show him that she put him first.

She waved the conductor on and turned to Georgette. "What happened?"

The train doors closed, the whistle blasted again and the train drew forward, gathering speed with every yard.

Georgette tucked her arm through Catherine's and dragged her toward the exit. "He was walking down the hill to see you at Lake House when the brake on an auto failed and struck him down."

"An auto." Catherine pictured the heavy machine barreling down the hill, striking him, crushing him. "Who-whose auto was it?"

Georgette sighed with a catch in the middle of the exhalation. "Ours."

Tristram raised his lids to see Catherine gazing down at him with eyes as soft as velvet, her hand holding his. He managed a smile. "I needed to see you."

"I'm here now."

He closed his eyes again, aching all over from bruised

and broken ribs, a sprained wrist and ankle, and more bruises. About the only part of him not hit by the speeding automobile was his head, spared when he dove headfirst into a snowbank.

One more attempt on his life, this one coming too close to be brushed aside for the sake of not making his father angry. The culprit had to have known he had left the Selkirks and headed down the hill.

He knew the answer. Of course he did. But Dr. Rushmore had made him drink what felt like a gallon of chloral hydrate for the pain, and his brain felt too fogged to think.

"I'll stay here as long as I can." Catherine drew his hand to her cheek, then rested it on the coverlet again. "So are Georgette and Ambrose with you."

"Florian? Where?" Tristram levered himself up on one elbow. "Where is Florian?"

"Later." She smoothed hair back from his brow with a cool hand. "When you're more awake."

"Where is Florian?" He would ask the question until she answered.

"May as well tell him." Ambrose's voice rumbled across the room.

She sighed. "Florian seems to have eloped with my sister."

"Did he?" Tristram started to chuckle. A stab of pain sliced through his ribs and he stopped. "He'd better marry her or I'll take drastic measures."

"He'll marry her." Ambrose sounded disgruntled. "Some men enjoy charmed lives. Florian gets his heiress. You get yours. Me, I get nothing."

"I have little enough to offer a bride." Tristram managed to open his eyes wide enough to look into Catherine's. "Perhaps a true title in a few years, but no money."

"You could still find the thief by your father's deadline." Her smile was probably meant to be encouraging.

He shook his head, making it swim, but held his ground. "I've given up on that. I can't risk my life just to impress him."

Across the room, Georgette emitted a little sob.

He wished she weren't there. He had tried to talk to her there at the racket club. But she had given him a curt, "I understand," and climbed into the automobile with several other ladies. He had walked, forming a speech to her in his head. He recalled most of it, but his limbs felt too heavy, his mind too slow for speech. His eyelids drifted shut, but sleep was too easy an escape.

"Georgette? Please... Here?"

A rustle of fabric, the tap of heels on the floor and she stood on the opposite side from Catherine. "I'm here." She sniffed.

"Thank you. I'm sorry." He tried to breathe, winced and pressed on. "I value the friendship you've offered me. And I should not have let you think there could be anything between us. Please forgive me."

"You're forgiven." Georgette sighed. "I should have known from the night of the ball when I saw you talking to Catherine."

"I never intended," Catherine blurted. "I tried to stay away, to keep him away." She lowered her head. "I tried not to love him."

"I know you did, Catherine." Georgette hastened to Catherine's side and embraced her. "Things are different this time. You didn't even particularly like Edwin. You just wanted the prize. But now— You truly love Tristram. I don't think you would have kissed him in front of everyone if you didn't."

Tristram smiled. No, she would not have.

"But you... Again." Catherine wiped her eyes. "It's not right."

"It wouldn't be if I loved him like you do. But, as with Bisterne, I wanted to marry Tristram so I wouldn't be stranded here. So now my parents will have to let me travel somewhere besides the city with them." Georgette kissed Catherine's cheek, then Tristram's. "You are both my dear friends. As the Lord brought you two together, I know He has someone for me." She embraced Catherine again, then headed for the door.

"When you least expect it." Still smiling, he let the medication take over his mind again and woke sometime later to the murmur of voices.

"If his sister-in-law has a boy, you'll have nothing but a useless courtesy title." Ambrose spoke with a sneer to his voice. "His father is going to cut him off. Tris has been such an embarrassment. He has no standing in society. They all know he was asked to leave the military, even if we pretend he resigned on his own."

"Do you think that matters to me? I had a title once. I haven't seen it's brought me anything but misery."

"And you think he loves you, not your trust fund? Ha." Ambrose's bark of laughter held no mirth.

Tristram stirred, wishing for the strength to shout Ambrose down.

Catherine's hand tightened on his, almost as though warning him to remain quiet. "Money isn't important to Tristram. He's wanted his father's respect and has given it up for me."

"Love and money." Ambrose sounded more sad than bitter now. "Some men get everything and some of us nothing."

"Perhaps you need to find work for yourself," Catherine said, "even if it's not right for an English gentleman. It's not that way here."

"I don't know how to work unless I join Estelle and Florian making music, for what? Coins tossed to them on the street? But then, Estelle has enough money not to stoop to that sort of life."

"If my parents allow her to have it."

"They will, and Florian won't mind about the jewels anymore, either, but his brother and my uncle will never give up on getting back what's theirs." Ambrose began to pace, his heels clunking on the wooden boards, then silent on the rug, and back again to the boards. "I'm only good at gaming."

Catherine smoothed her fingers over Tristram's. "And spending it or losing it again. You must have won a fortune from my husband. Did he not pay you?"

"Oh, he paid me—in false coin. That is to say—" Ambrose didn't say what he intended. He collapsed onto a chair.

And the drug washed from Tristram's brain as though a tidal wave had swept it clear. He rose on his elbow and grasped Catherine's wrist. "False…coin." Each word hurt to speak. "False coin."

Her eyes wide, she stared back at him. "As in false jewels."

"No, no, I didn't!" Ambrose cried. "I couldn't. The jewelry was in the safe."

"No, it wasn't, was it?" Catherine rose and walked to stand with her back to the door.

"Don't," Tristram gasped out. "He's dangerous. He tried to kill me."

"I did not. You're family. You're my friend." Ambrose shook so badly Tristram saw it from across the room. "I wouldn't have let you die. I just wanted to scare you off hunting the jewels. I wanted you to think it was Catherine or… I didn't try to kill you. You weren't truly dangerous to me."

"I am one more barrier to the title," Tristram said between shallow breaths.

"That auto nearly killed him." Catherine's tone was as hard as real diamonds.

"It got away from me. I thought he'd get out of the way in time." Ambrose's pitch rose like someone on the edge of hysteria or an act of violence. "I've been sitting vigil here because I was afraid. I'm not a murderer."

"No, just greedy." Tristram's eyes burned. His heart ached with pain worse than his broken ribs. "If you weren't family, I'd have worked it out sooner. But we've been friends all our lives. You didn't shun me when I came back from South Africa." Spent, he sank back onto his pillows, a lump rising in his throat. "Suspected Catherine. Suspected Florian. Believe me, Ambrose, if I legally could, I'd give you the title. I don't want it."

"Well, you have it." A hard edge rang through Ambrose's words. "A telegram came yesterday morning. Her ladyship, the vicountess, has safely delivered a girl, albeit early."

Tristram's heart squeezed. "I'm sorry. I don't want it."

"No, but you get it. You get everything. And I—" Ambrose sprang to his feet. His chair crashed to the floor as he sprang toward Tristram.

"Run!" he managed to gasp out before Ambrose pressed a pillow over his face.

He clawed at his cousin's hand. He may as well have tried to move a boulder with a teaspoon. The pillow remained, blocking off breath, sending spots dancing before his eyes and blood roaring in his ears.

A scream and another crash penetrated the waterfall blackness. And the pillow sailed away. Air rushed into his lungs so fast his ribs protested.

"Tristram." Catherine rested her hands on either side of his face. "Look at me."

He looked at her. He smiled.

"Thank You, Jesus." She was breathing hard and weeping, but smiling. "I hit him over the head."

"How fitting. Better ring for help."

But the door flew open and Mrs. VanDorn, Georgette, Pierce and three footmen burst into the room. Confusion reigned for several minutes, and in the end, the footmen carried Ambrose away and Pierce called the police. Through it all, Catherine stood beside Tristram, holding his hand until quiet settled over them.

"You can't stay alone with him in here," Mrs. VanDorn said. "Not more than a minute or two alone." She left, allowing the door to hang open an inch or two.

Tristram turned to Catherine and gazed into her lovely eyes. "I'm sorry, Catherine. I know it's not what you want, but I do love you. Will you marry me and live in England with a future marquess?"

"I love you enough to live with you under any name in any country."

Epilogue

A wedding in very best taste for a widow would be a ceremony in a small church or chapel, a few flowers or palms in the chancel the only decoration, and two to four ushers. There are no ribboned-off seats, as only very intimate friends are asked. The bride wears an afternoon street dress and hat. Her dress for a church ceremony should be more conventional than if she were married at home, where she could wear a semi-evening gown and substitute a headdress for a hat. She could even wear a veil if it is colored and does not suggest the bridal white one.

Emily Price Post

For once, Estelle did not insist on providing the music. Carrying a bouquet of yellow roses and wearing an indigo gown and wide-brimmed hat trimmed in indigo ribbons, she stepped out of the music room and headed up the aisle made by the rows of chairs set up in the VanDorns' drawing room. Forty friends and family turned to watch her, some with disapproving frowns, some with raised eyebrows, but most smiling.

No smile could be as wide as Catherine's as she clutched her father's arm and watched her beautiful, talented sister glide toward the fireplace, where her new husband stood as best man to Catherine's groom.

"Even if she did elope," Catherine murmured to Papa, "you should be proud of her."

"We are." He cleared his throat. "Even if they went all the way to Virginia to get married so they didn't need our permission. If she'd waited a bit, we might have given our permission."

"It's the *might have* given your permission that was the difficulty." Catherine patted his arm. "They'll make you proud."

"As traveling musicians?" He shook his head. "Outrageous."

It was rather, but Catherine had never seen two people so happy—except for she and and her beloved.

Only three things brought them sadness on their glorious day. Georgette was not there to be Catherine's attendant, as she and a hired companion had sailed for Rio de Janeiro the previous week. She intended to explore the Amazon, the furthest life from Tuxedo Park she could imagine. Far from seeking freedom, Ambrose waited to learn whether he would stand trial in America or England, as he had committed crimes in both. Catherine and Tristram prayed for his salvation daily.

The biggest source of Tristram's regret was that he hadn't heard a word from his father since telegraphing the news regarding Ambrose six weeks earlier. Catherine prayed that the marquess would at least acknowledge their wedding. Doubt that her prayer would be answered rose upon occasion, but she thanked the Lord for His will working in their lives and held on to hope even as the string quartet played the wedding music behind her, signaling her moment had come to walk toward her groom.

The minute she stepped through the drawing room doorway, she felt his eyes upon her. Along the length of the chamber, she met his dark green gaze and held it. The closer she drew to him, the more she read tenderness, love and approval in his eyes. She hoped he liked her gold satin gown and wide-brimmed hat with filmy gold veiling floating from the brim. She certainly approved of his black suit, white shirt and inability to tame his cowlick. That errant curl made her smile.

She reached Tristram's side and handed Estelle her bouquet of creamy roses. Papa set her hand in Tristram's and stepped back to make room for the pastor.

"Dearly beloved, we are gathered here—"

The drawing room door flew open. "So sorry to interrupt."

Everyone turned toward the newcomer, a tall, elegant man in late middle age with light brown hair going gray and familiar features.

Catherine caught her breath and looked up at Tristram. Barely healed from his injuries, he had grown pale and swayed forward half a step.

She slipped her arm around his waist. "Are you all right?"

He shook his head. "Father, what are you doing here?"

"You did send me an invitation." The Marquess of Cothbridge strode up the aisle and gripped Tristram's shoulder. "I tried to get here sooner, but it's difficult getting across the North Atlantic this time of year. You couldn't have waited until spring?" He glanced at Catherine and bowed. "But of course not. How do you do, my lady?"

Catherine opened her mouth, but no words emerged.

"Better if I sit down and let this ceremony continue?"

"Yes, my lord."

His brows arched nearly to his hairline at her forthright response, but he merely inclined his head and accepted the seat her brother had vacated for him.

"Continue," Tristram directed the pastor in a voice that quivered with what some might have thought anger, others distress, and Catherine knew from the faintest twitch at the corner of his mouth, to be suppressed laughter.

His face bemused, the pastor continued with the ceremony. Tristram and Catherine spoke their vows and, against custom, exchanged rings. Then, with Tristram's hand covering Catherine's where it rested on his forearm, they recessed to the drawing room door to greet the well-wishers.

While the guests filed into the dining room for the wedding tea, the marquess held back so that he was the last to approach them. He bowed, then gripped both their hands. "I owe you both apologies." He cleared his throat.

They gazed back at him.

"For what, sir?" Tristram asked.

"For being ashamed of you. For sending you into danger. For not listening when you tried to tell me about your work with the former soldiers. When I learned you were nearly killed—" He scowled. "From others, not you, I must note, I realized I'd, uh, been so determined to have a son who did the things I thought would make me proud that I didn't realize I had a son who had already done things to make me proud." He kissed Catherine's cheek. "I like your wife. She spoke her vows like your mother did—like she means every word."

"I do." Catherine smiled, her heart swelling with joy.

Tristram slipped his arm around her shoulders. "And I love her rather intensely, the more for the fact she has put my accusing her of theft and worse behind us."

"Then I have hope that you can put everything I've said and done to you behind you," the marquess said.

Tristram reached his free hand out to his father. "I already have."

His father clasped the proffered hand.

"Now, if you will excuse me, sir, I'd like a few minutes alone with my wife."

"The guests are waiting for us," Catherine said.

But she didn't protest when, his arm still around her, Tristram led Catherine up the steps to the conservatory. With the guests in the dining room below, the room was dark, save for outside lights glowing off the snow. "I am going to miss this room."

"Why this one?" Catherine rested her head on his shoulder.

"I think maybe I fell in love with you here overlooking the lake and the trees that first day I came to see you."

She laughed and slipped her arm around him. "It was so cold I thought I'd freeze you out of my life."

"Instead, you warmed me to my heart." He turned from the frosty landscape to his radiant bride and kissed her. "I love you now and forever."

* * * * *

REQUEST YOUR FREE BOOKS!

2 FREE INSPIRATIONAL NOVELS
PLUS 2
FREE
MYSTERY GIFTS

Love Inspired

YES! Please send me 2 FREE Love Inspired® novels and my 2 FREE mystery gifts (gifts are worth about $10). After receiving them, if I don't wish to receive any more books, I can return the shipping statement marked "cancel." If I don't cancel, I will receive 6 brand-new novels every month and be billed just $4.74 per book in the U.S. or $5.24 per book in Canada. That's a savings of at least 21% off the cover price. It's quite a bargain! Shipping and handling is just 50¢ per book in the U.S. and 75¢ per book in Canada.* I understand that accepting the 2 free books and gifts places me under no obligation to buy anything. I can always return a shipment and cancel at any time. Even if I never buy another book, the two free books and gifts are mine to keep forever.

105/305 IDN F49N

Name _____ (PLEASE PRINT) _____

Address _____ Apt. # _____

City _____ State/Prov. _____ Zip/Postal Code _____

Signature (if under 18, a parent or guardian must sign)

Mail to the Harlequin® Reader Service:
IN U.S.A.: P.O. Box 1867, Buffalo, NY 14240-1867
IN CANADA: P.O. Box 609, Fort Erie, Ontario L2A 5X3

**Are you a subscriber to Love Inspired books
and want to receive the larger-print edition?
Call 1-800-873-8635 or visit www.ReaderService.com.**

* Terms and prices subject to change without notice. Prices do not include applicable taxes. Sales tax applicable in N.Y. Canadian residents will be charged applicable taxes. Offer not valid in Quebec. This offer is limited to one order per household. Not valid for current subscribers to Love Inspired books. All orders subject to credit approval. Credit or debit balances in a customer's account(s) may be offset by any other outstanding balance owed by or to the customer. Please allow 4 to 6 weeks for delivery. Offer available while quantities last.

Your Privacy—The Harlequin® Reader Service is committed to protecting your privacy. Our Privacy Policy is available online at www.ReaderService.com or upon request from the Harlequin Reader Service.
We make a portion of our mailing list available to reputable third parties that offer products we believe may interest you. If you prefer that we not exchange your name with third parties, or if you wish to clarify or modify your communication preferences, please visit us at www.ReaderService.com/consumerchoice or write to us at Harlequin Reader Service Preference Service, P.O. Box 9062, Buffalo, NY 14269. Include your complete name and address.

LIDIR13R

REQUEST YOUR FREE BOOKS!

2 FREE INSPIRATIONAL NOVELS
PLUS 2
FREE
MYSTERY GIFTS

Love Inspired
HISTORICAL
INSPIRATIONAL HISTORICAL ROMANCE

YES! Please send me 2 FREE Love Inspired® Historical novels and my 2 FREE mystery gifts (gifts are worth about $10). After receiving them, if I don't wish to receive any more books, I can return the shipping statement marked "cancel." If I don't cancel, I will receive 4 brand-new novels every month and be billed just $4.74 per book in the U.S. or $5.24 per book in Canada. That's a savings of at least 21% off the cover price. It's quite a bargain! Shipping and handling is just 50¢ per book in the U.S. and 75¢ per book in Canada.* I understand that accepting the 2 free books and gifts places me under no obligation to buy anything. I can always return a shipment and cancel at any time. Even if I never buy another book, the two free books and gifts are mine to keep forever.

102/302 IDN F5CY

Name	(PLEASE PRINT)	
Address		Apt. #
City	State/Prov.	Zip/Postal Code

Signature (if under 18, a parent or guardian must sign)

Mail to the **Harlequin® Reader Service:**
IN U.S.A.: P.O. Box 1867, Buffalo, NY 14240-1867
IN CANADA: P.O. Box 609, Fort Erie, Ontario L2A 5X3

Want to try two free books from another series?
Call 1-800-873-8635 or visit www.ReaderService.com.

* Terms and prices subject to change without notice. Prices do not include applicable taxes. Sales tax applicable in N.Y. Canadian residents will be charged applicable taxes. Offer not valid in Quebec. This offer is limited to one order per household. Not valid for current subscribers to Love Inspired Historical books. All orders subject to credit approval. Credit or debit balances in a customer's account(s) may be offset by any other outstanding balance owed by or to the customer. Please allow 4 to 6 weeks for delivery. Offer available while quantities last.

Your Privacy—The Harlequin® Reader Service is committed to protecting your privacy. Our Privacy Policy is available online at www.ReaderService.com or upon request from the Harlequin Reader Service.

We make a portion of our mailing list available to reputable third parties that offer products we believe may interest you. If you prefer that we not exchange your name with third parties, or if you wish to clarify or modify your communication preferences, please visit us at www.ReaderService.com/consumerchoice or write to us at Harlequin Reader Service Preference Service, P.O. Box 9062, Buffalo, NY 14269. Include your complete name and address.

LIHDIR13R

Reader Service.com

Manage your account online!

- Review your order history
- Manage your payments
- Update your address

---

*We've designed
the Harlequin® Reader Service
website just for you.*

Enjoy all the features!

- Reader excerpts from any series
- Respond to mailings and
  special monthly offers
- Discover new series available to you
- Browse the Bonus Bucks catalog
- Share your feedback

Visit us at:

ReaderService.com

RS13